FRIDAY
NIGHT
MASSACRE

Friday Night Massacre contains graphic content and is recommended for regular readers of horror novels.

A list of content warnings is located at the back of this book and online at my website:

https://www.michaelpatrickhicks.com/ friday-night-massacre

PRAISE FOR MICHAEL PATRICK HICKS

BROKEN SHELLS

"A fun and nasty little novella...If you're a big creature-feature fan (digging on works like Adam Cesare's *Video Night* or Hunter Shea's *They Rise*) you're going to love this book."
— Glenn Rolfe, author of *Becoming* and *Blood and Rain*

"An adrenaline-fueled, no punches pulled, onslaught of gruesome action! Highly recommended!"
— Horror After Dark

"Lightning fast...high octane fun."
— Unnerving Magazine

"*Broken Shells* is a blood-soaked, tense novella that is sure to appeal to a wide variety of horror fans, especially those that dig an old-school feel in their novels."
— The Horror Bookshelf

"The very definition of a page-turner. Michael Patrick Hicks delivers right-between-the-eyes terror."
— The Haunted Reading Room

"Unnerving! ... It truly is the perfect blend of gore, horror and action."
— PopHorror.com

"Michael Patrick Hicks has managed, in only 120 pages, to craft a terrifying, steamroller of a story. The author makes you immediately connect with the main character Antoine, who is down on his luck and just looking for a possible break. When Antoine

is thrust into the dark, you are along for the ride, whether you like it or not. And in the dark is where this story shines. Hicks makes you feel dread, like the walls are closing in as you read."

— One-Legged Reviews

"Hicks does a fine job of emotionally grasping the reader with his character creation. You'll come for the story of survival, and stay for the darkness and gore. If you enjoy extremely gruesome creature horror and pitch black underground tunnels, then *Broken Shells* is right up your alley."

— FanFiAddict

MASS HYSTERIA

"Brutal horror. Raw. Animalistic. I couldn't put it down!"

— Armand Rosamilia, author of the Dying Days series

"*Mass Hysteria* is a hell of a brutal, end of the world free for all. A terrifying vision of a future gone mad with bloodlust, *Mass Hysteria* will haunt your nightmares."

— Hunter Shea, author of *Creature* and
We Are Always Watching

"A mindfuck of a story masquerading as an apocalyptic thriller. Once it takes its mask off, it's *Night of the Comet* meets *Pink Flamingos.*"

— Chris Sorensen, author of *The Nightmare Room*

"There are horror novels, and then there are HORROR novels. You know, the ones with blood dripping off the letters (and pages) and sinking deep into the pit of your soul, causing you to question the decency of humanity and existence itself. *Mass Hysteria*, by Michael Patrick Hicks, certainly falls into this latter

category. Masterful storytelling, but NOT for the faint of heart. You've been warned."

— The Behrg, author of *Housebroken* and The Creation series

"Fun, horrible fun, from start to finish."

— Horror Novel Reviews

"It's fast paced, action-packed, and bloody. Really, almost everything a horror gore-hound could want. ... Undeniably talented, Michael Patrick Hicks shows evidence of a rather deliciously depraved mind..."

— SciFi & Scary

"*Mass Hysteria* was a brutal horror novel, which reminded me of the horror being written in the late 70's and, (all of the), 80's. Books like James Herbert's *The Rats* or Guy N. Smith's *The Night of the Crabs*. There are a lot of similarities to those classics here-the fast paced action going from scene to scene-with many gory deaths and other sick events. In fact, I think *Mass Hysteria* beats out those books in its sheer horrific brutality."

— Char's Horror Corner

"I'm telling you now, this book isn't for readers with weak stomachs. It is brutal in all the right ways."

— Cedar Hollow Horror Reviews

"If you are an aficionado of author Richard Laymon, you undoubtedly will like this book. This is horror at its bloodiest, guttiest and most shocking."

— Cheryl Stout, Amazon Top Reviewer

ALSO BY MICHAEL PATRICK HICKS

Friday Night Massacre

Broken Shells: A Subterranean Horror Novella

Mass Hysteria

THE SALEM HAWLEY SERIES

The Resurrectionists (Book 1)

Borne of the Deep (Book 2)

DRMR SERIES

Convergence (A DRMR Novel, Book 1)

Emergence (A DRMR Novel, Book 2)

Preservation (A DRMR Short Story)

SHORT STORIES

The Marque

Black Site

Let Go

Revolver

Consumption

NON-FICTION

The Horror Book Review Digest Vol. I

The Horror Book Review Digest Vol. II

FRIDAY NIGHT MASSACRE

MICHAEL PATRICK HICKS

FRIDAY NIGHT MASSACRE
Copyright © 2021 by Michael Patrick Hicks

High Fever Books
First edition: February 2021

Edited by Red Adept Editing
http://redadeptpublishing.com/

Cover artwork by Kealan Patrick Burke
http://www.elderlemondesign.com

Printed in the United States of America

ISBN-13: 978-1-947570-15-3
ISBN-13: 978-1-947570-16-0 (ebook)

*To the eighty-one million Americans who pulled us
back from the brink—thank you.*

"When you're a star, they let you do it. You can do anything. … Grab 'em by the pussy. You can do anything."

— Donald J. Trump, 45th president of
the United States

"If we nominate Trump, we will get destroyed… and we will deserve it."

— Senator Lindsey Graham

"If there's one thing I've learned with 35 years in the horror business, it's that evil does not go down without a fight."

— Barbara Crampton

COLERIDGE RETURNS
TO WHITE HOUSE

December 27, 2020

WASHINGTON—Two days after being airlifted aboard *Marine One* to Walter Reed National Military Medical Center for emergency medical treatment for COVID-19, President Coleridge has returned to the White House.

In a brief statement delivered from the staircase of the South Portico entrance, Coleridge again dismissed the novel coronavirus as a hoax perpetuated by liberal media.

"I don't know," he said. "Maybe I'm immune. I have a very good immune system and am in perfect health. I don't know what they're talking about."

Although Coleridge seemed, at times, to struggle for breath and appeared tired, he insisted, "Look at me. I am a perfect human specimen. I'm strong. I feel good. The best I've ever been, I can tell you that right now."

Since it was first detected in the United States in February, more than ten million Americans have become infected with COVID-19. Over three hundred thousand deaths have been attributed to the virus. Critics of President Coleridge claim he is directly responsible for that high casualty rate, blaming his slow response to the growing pandemic and the anti-mask messages that he has routinely delivered during his numerous rallies this past year.

With Inauguration Day only weeks away, Coleridge was again asked if he intends to peacefully transfer power to his Democratic challenger, Marcus Barnett. Barnett edged out the incumbent in November, winning the race with 306 electoral votes to Coleridge's 232. Despite failing to secure the 270 electoral votes needed to win a second term in office, Coleridge has yet to concede defeat, even after numerous losses when attempting to overturn the election results in court.

"This is fraud on the American republic. This is an embarrassment to our country, and we will not stand for it. We will not stand for it," Coleridge said, continuing to insist voter fraud. "We won this election."

Since November and without evidence, the president has repeated his claims that there were major problems with the voting and ballot counting in cities all across America. Republicans swiftly filed lawsuits in several states to contest election results. Those were dismissed by judges almost immediately. In the weeks since, Coleridge has again and again demanded on Twitter that ballots in several highly contested battleground states be purged due to incorrect counting.

Proper tallying of votes was made more difficult this election season due to unusually long lines at polling stations as voters waited for hours to cast their ballots, and a virtual flood of mail-in ballots were delivered to local clerks' offices across the country. These efforts were further hampered by violent protests in several contested states where the president's supporters attempted to halt the counting of legitimate votes.

Coleridge, who registered for an absentee ballot in Florida earlier this year, has been a staunch adversary of mail-in voting, claiming the process would lead to widespread voter fraud. However, no proof of fraud has yet materialized to support the president's assertions.

Barnett's campaign manager, Suzanne Sloane, issued a statement calling Coleridge's latest comments "yet another outrageous and direct attack on American principles."

"Never before in the history of this country has an American president fought so hard to undermine our national institutions and strip the American people of their voice," Sloane said. "Every vote cast will count because that is what the American people themselves and the laws of this country—laws that protect every American's constitutional right to vote—demand. And rightly so."

Standing outside the White House Residence, Coleridge urged his supporters, "Stand by, okay? We're working on it. Somebody's gotta do something. Stand by. Be ready.

"I think," Coleridge added, "that when the votes are counted, properly this time, because we're going to make sure it's correct, that every vote is counted right, and by that, I mean that it's counted correctly and properly, you'll see. You'll see. This is my country. I'm the president. I don't think there's any doubt about that. So be ready. Boozy Barnett hasn't won anything. I'm not going anywhere. Anywhere. You'll see."

COLERIDGE LOST—BUT DON'T EXPECT HIM TO GO AWAY

Dec. 30, 2020

Although he has less than a month left in office, don't expect President Tyler Coleridge—or his supporters—to quietly disappear.

Despite losing the election, Coleridge will surely remain a disruptive and powerful force in American life. Having received over seventy-four million votes, up more than 10 million votes from 2016 and commanded 47% of the popular vote, he has retained the support of nearly half of the public despite four years of scandal, setbacks, impeachment, and the brutal coronavirus outbreak that has killed nearly three hundred and twenty thousand Americans.

We've already seen him leverage his political power to carry out personal revenge against his opponents numerous times over the course of his first and only term. Shortly after losing the election, Coleridge fired Dr. Martin Fiero, the government's top infectious diseases expert, in the middle of a pandemic, just as infection rates began soaring once again. In the last few weeks, we've seen him eliminate FBI Director Dean Wright and other senior officials who failed to carry out Coleridge's wishes to investigate his opponent, Marcus Barnett, during the battle for the White House. Yesterday, via a tweet, Coleridge terminated Cybersecurity and Infrastructure Security Agency chief Roger Galli-

gan following Galligan's announcement that there "is no evidence that any voting system deleted or lost votes, or was in any way compromised." Sources within the White House are already anticipating additional firings of those whom Coleridge sees as disloyal, viewing the president's actions as an on-going series of Friday and Saturday Night Massacres that have been a staple of Coleridge's presidency.

Although that presidency will soon be over, Coleridge has already promised America he won't be going anywhere. He has long toyed with starting his own television network to compete with Fox News, and his one-hundred-million-strong Twitter following gives him a loud bullhorn to continue being a powerful voice on the right. It's likely he will use that online platform to become a Republican kingmaker in the years to come.

What will he do with all of that influence once he's freed of the White House?

"It's clear from the election that this president has a massive following, and he doesn't plan to just disappear from public life like some other past presidents," said former Sen. Robert Owen of Ohio.

(Continued on Page A19)

ONE

TYLER COLERIDGE'S FAMILY WAS GATHERED in the bedroom of the president's private residence. Hands joined, they encircled the death bed of the most powerful man on the planet.

Only a few days prior, Coleridge had returned home after a weekend in the hospital. He'd spent the ride back to the White House having his hair primped and makeup applied, wanting to look strong and victorious. The act had worked, and the media and the American people had eaten it up like sweet, sweet candy. It had also exhausted Coleridge so badly that he'd almost collapsed on the other side of the South Portico entrance. If his son, David, hadn't been there to help keep him propped up, he would have.

David and his brother, Stephen, had helped the man to the elevator and, from there, to the second-floor bedroom, where Coleridge, coughing and wheezing himself red-faced, fell into bed. Their step-

mother—Coleridge's third trophy wife, Melanie—came with oxygen and helped to fit the mask over Tyler's face.

"Sleep now," she'd ordered. Coleridge rarely ever listened to his wife about anything, but in this one instance, he had nodded and acquiesced. He was out in less than a minute and had slept well into the following day.

After waking up close to noon, upset that he'd missed *Fox & Friends*, Coleridge eased himself out of bed. David and Stephen had been waiting for him in the living room, and they hurried to his side to help him with the newly prescribed walker. Coleridge was weak and shaky, and even in spite of the many hours of sleep, he still looked the worse for wear. He looked frail, his skin unnaturally pale, save for his reddened cheeks. His thinning blond hair hung limply over his forehead, and David watched as the oxygen mask clouded over and cleared, clouded and cleared, clouded and cleared. He knew, then, that his father wouldn't be making it out of the residence.

He was right too. Coleridge hadn't managed to stray farther than the living room, and although he insisted he wanted to at least stand on the balcony, the walk there was simply too taxing.

When the White House physician arrived to check on the president, she was summarily and angrily dismissed. After coughing up a storm, Coleridge pulled the mask down far enough to shout at her that he wasn't sick and to get out of the room, until he was left gasping for air. Dr. Roth later informed the press, as instructed, that the president was in good spirits and that his health was improving. Coleridge watched, bitterly and half asleep, from the television in his bedroom.

Following a three-hour nap, Coleridge removed the oxygen mask. Breathing on his own proved to be a laborious effort, and his gasps came in short, shallow bursts that renewed his persistent

cough. For the next three days, Melanie and her sons sat outside the bedroom in the West Sitting Hall, as if keeping a vigil. Upon hearing his father's ragged intake of air and what sounded like the grinding of rocks deep in his chest, David decided that was exactly what they were doing.

Melanie took him water, David and Stephen following dutifully. She held the glass to Coleridge, and he took it in both hands. Drinking weakly, he looked like a toddler learning how to use a sippy cup. Arms shaking, he handed it back, and his head sank into the pillow. His eyes were glassy, and it seemed as if he had trouble focusing on his wife.

"I think it's time," he gasped. He looked like he'd just run a marathon.

Melanie, hands clasped in front of her, simply nodded.

"Evelyn… get Evelyn here," Coleridge said.

David noticed the president had failed to ask for either of his other daughters or his youngest son, eleven-year-old Maddock. Then again, he'd always had a special relationship with Evelyn. She was Daddy's little girl. The favorite.

"I'll call her," David said, removing his cell phone from an inner pocket of his suit jacket. When she answered on the third ring, he remembered his father's words and said only, "It's time." He knew Evelyn had been following the news and knew exactly what those two simple words meant.

"She's coming," he said, returning to Coleridge's bedside. He took his father's limp, greasy hand between both of his and brought it to his forehead. "She was doing that photo shoot for *Vogue*, but she'll be up soon."

"She shoulda been," Coleridge sputtered, "in *Penthouse*. Like her mom." Tyler offered a weak smile to Melanie, his eyes not quite able

to find hers.

David laughed good-naturedly, nodding his head in agreement. "Well, maybe one day, Pops." The least he could do was give the old man some measure of hope.

"Put on Dick Clark," Coleridge said, pointing his chin at the television.

David was on the verge of reminding the seventy-six-year-old elder that Clark had died ages ago, then he remembered what day it was.

"*New Year's Rockin' Eve*? You got it."

They all sat and watched as snow fell on an empty Times Square and a small gathering of socially distanced celebrities partied inside a New York TV studio. In an effort to help curb the spread of the coronavirus, the New Year's Eve celebration had gone virtual, something Coleridge had grumbled about to a booing audience in one of the last rallies before his health took a turn for the worse. In DC, it was only bitterly cold and windy. Seeing the profusion of surgical masks and covered faces on the small group of hired dancers shaking their asses for the live band, Coleridge scoffed, spurring on yet another coughing fit.

"Burkas," he said. "Next thing you know, they'll all be wearing burkas. Everyone'll be walking around looking like fucking ragheads."

Stephen put a reassuring hand on Coleridge's shoulder and squeezed gently, trying to calm him down. "It's okay, Dad," he said soothingly, even as his father made noises like he was gargling rocks and something was breaking apart deep inside him.

David checked his watch. *How much longer is this going to go on? Where the* Christ *is Evelyn?*

Bored of Seacrest's lame jokes and the awful musical acts ABC

had booked, David stood and made his way to the kitchen. He brewed a fresh pot of coffee, in for the makings of a long night, then scrounged up some lunch meat from the fridge. Not bothering with a sandwich, he ate the cold cuts straight out of the small plastic container. He washed it down with a Diet Pepsi then wiped his mouth with the back of his wrist.

Although Coleridge hadn't asked for Diana and Christie, David called them anyway, giving them the same message he'd given Evelyn. Both promised to be there within the hour. Then he went down the hall to the East Bedroom and rapped on the door even as he was opening it. He heard the rustling of movement and an abrupt moan, which was quickly silenced. Maddock's face was flushed, only his head sticking out from beneath the thick fleece blanket of his bed.

"Quit jerking off, you little shit. Put your dick away and meet us in the bedroom. It's almost time."

"I'll be there in a minute," the eleven-year-old said.

"Yeah, whatever," David said, putting his back to the boy. He could feel the beginnings of a headache rising behind his eyes and knew he was going to need something stronger than coffee and Diet Pepsi.

He went back to the kitchen, poured a mug of coffee, and added a healthy splash of whiskey. Then he added a second. He savored the long, slow sip, closing his eyes at the flush of pleasant heat that warmed him from the inside. That was so much better.

And just in time, he thought, hearing the elevator ding. Evelyn had arrived, at long last, along with her sisters. Diana and Christie were both fairly attractive women, but next to Evelyn, they looked like frumpy, used-up alley whores. Even though he was her older brother, David could easily understand why Dad favored Evelyn so much. He couldn't help but notice the first three buttons of her

blouse were undone, the plunging neckline revealing a triangular cut of flesh that drew his eyes toward her large breasts.

Daddy was right, he thought, not for the first time. *She really should have been in porn.*

He licked his lips as he approached and gave her a lingering hug, breathing in the sweet, flowery scent of her shampoo and perfume, ignoring his other two sisters completely. One hand lingered just above the swell of her ass.

"I'm sorry I'm late," Evelyn said. "I didn't miss it, did I?"

"No, it's early yet. We got time. How was *Vogue*?"

Evelyn shrugged. "The photographer was a fucking amateur, but what do you expect from that rag?"

Maddock came out of his room in disheveled pajamas then went to hug his sisters.

"I hope your hands are clean," David said. Maddock went red-faced again, and David elaborated for the recently arrived women. "He was spanking it five minutes ago. Probably just got his spunk all over your furs."

"You're so gross," Diana said. A foul look of contempt crossed her face. She ruffled Maddock's hair and gave him an air kiss. David gave them both the middle finger and led Evelyn back to the master bedroom.

In the time he'd been away, Melanie had worked on getting everything set up. Although the lights were off, the bedroom was bright from nearly a dozen candles and the glow of the television. The TV remained on, no doubt at Father's insistence. Watching the New Year's ball drop was one of his favorite traditions, largely because ABC was always sure to position their cameras at the perfect angle to catch the Coleridge Enterprises tower in the background.

Stephen offered to get food and drinks for everyone while

they waited, but most demurred, Coleridge's daughters insisting they couldn't eat at a time like this. Their emotions blanketed the room, but it wasn't sadness that hung in the air. *Anticipation*, David thought; that was more like it.

The New Year's celebration wore on, and Coleridge's condition continued to deteriorate. At some point during the long night, he'd dozed off. David wondered idly where Melanie had put the oxygen mask and tank, but he brushed those thoughts aside. It was too late, anyway.

Coleridge's breathing grew more and more labored as the hours stretched on.

"It won't be long now," Melanie said, a hint of a promise in her voice. She could have been talking about the buildup to the count-down to 2021, but everyone knew otherwise. Coleridge's chest bare-ly rose and fell, and his pale, clammy face had a sunken look about it. His cheeks had darkened, and thick, purple bags hung beneath both eyes.

"*Ten!… Nine!… Eight!…*" Ryan Seacrest chanted from his vir-tual Zoom studio.

Coleridge was dead before they hit five. David watched the old man's chest sink, hearing that noisome rattle of his final breath as his lips parted and the last gasp of air escaped his body.

"Happy New Year!"

David wiped at his eyes, but there were no tears. He stood and took his mother's hand. The seven of them spread out in a circle around the bed, each holding the hands of the people next to them.

"Close your eyes," Melanie said. A moment later, she began to speak, but David didn't understand any of the words. It was in the Old Language, as his stepmother called it, and he'd never learned Russian. He wasn't even sure he'd ever heard it spoken prior to this

night.

Eyes sealed tightly, he watched the flicker of lights dancing on the inside of his eyelids. He wanted to open them, but he forced them to remain sealed, even as a hot breeze washed over him. His face grew warm as a rank, humid moistness washed over his skin. He was revolted, but he kept his body as still as possible, just as he'd been instructed. He tightened his grip on Melanie's and Evelyn's hands, their palms sweating against his.

David squinted his eyes shut even more tightly against a brilliant flash of light, wind kicking up in the room powerfully enough to ruffle his hair. He could hear the *whoosh* of it, too loud, and it grew stronger, nearly knocking him back off his feet. But he stayed true, standing proudly against the strange turbulence as the ground shook beneath his feet. Something cracked loudly in the walls around him. The wind died abruptly, and the light faded.

Slowly, the noise of a New Year's Eve party came back to him. He drew in a deep breath then gagged. The air stank of rotten eggs and hot garbage.

"Everyone can open their eyes now," Melanie said, her voice softly accented. After all her years in America, she'd never lost that accent.

David took another breath; the air was suddenly clean and fresh. He breathed deeply a second time, feeling invigorated and strong. He laughed softly to himself then looked at Evelyn. She stared straight ahead, her full, luscious lips curled into a wicked smile.

President Tyler Coleridge sat comfortably in bed, propped up by a few pillows between his back and the headboard. He looked at his family then held his hands out to either side. He smiled, revealing a set of perfectly straight, perfectly white teeth that shone in the candlelight. His skin tone had taken on a healthier pallor, and he looked

rested, ready to go.

"Happy New Year," he said.

David laughed then gripped his father's foot through the bed-covers, giving it a hearty shake.

President Coleridge had died. President Coleridge now lived.

Time to get to work.

TWO

MIKE HUTCHINSON ARRIVED AT THE White House at exactly 8:00 a.m., just in time for the start of his shift. Hutchinson had once been prone to arriving ten to fifteen minutes early so that he would have additional time to apprise himself of the reports from the overnight detail, but he'd fallen out of habit over the years of serving President Coleridge. He was loath to admit it to anyone, even himself, but the less time he had to spend around that man, the better. The members of his administration were no better, and many were, in decorum-shattering displays of outright nepotism, directly related to the president.

Another thing Hutchinson would never admit, lest it stain his career with the United States Secret Service, was that he outright hated Coleridge. He kept that tidbit deeply buried, a secret he shared with absolutely no one. He'd served under two prior presidents over

the last sixteen years, and while both had their ups and downs in certain regards, Hutchinson did believe both men were fundamentally decent human beings at heart. While he hadn't always agreed with either of those men politically, both had been fair, caring, and compassionate men in his estimation. Coleridge, on the other hand, was a pile of human garbage shoved into a cheap suit. Hutchinson would have been hard-pressed to name even one redeeming feature about the man.

In fact, even after nearly four years, he was still shell-shocked that Coleridge had ever become president at all. Hutchinson remembered all too well waking up on a cold, rainy November morning after the election and turning on the news. He'd been gut punched by the results. How could America have elected such a man? All through his campaign, Coleridge had proved over and over just how unfit he was for office with his flagrant displays of racism, authoritarianism, narcissism, bigotry, sexism, and misogyny. Hutchinson had learned a lot about the real face of the United States of America that morning, and it had felt like he'd woken up in an alien land. Even four years later, he still felt like he was living in some perverse alternate reality, one that only barely resembled the America he'd grown up in.

The subsequent years were even worse. Coleridge had leveraged his political might to encourage his supporters to attack journalists and minorities, mocked the disabled, mused about his political rivals being assassinated or jailed without a trial, and in one startling display of treason, begged Russia to hack the then-Secretary of State in order to obtain her classified e-mails as well as the Democratic National Committee's computer servers and provide him with dirt on his rivals. He had mocked the Muslim family of a slain United States Army captain and called every one of the nation's service members losers and suckers. He'd ordered the construction of concentration

camps along the US-Mexico border, erected in lieu of Coleridge's promised wall to divide the two nations. Children were torn apart from their families and locked in crowded cages, denied even their most basic human rights, and left to starve, to die of treatable diseases, and to be raped by their guards. Women were subjected to forced hysterectomies for illegally crossing the border, like some kind of deranged medical experimentation at the hands of Josef Mengele.

Coleridge's entire tenure as president had been built on hate and division, a complete and utter refutation of his Republican predecessors' proclamations of being a uniter, not a divider. Coleridge was every inch the divider and proud of it. Sowing division and hate kept him at the top of the news hour, on the front pages of every newspaper in America, and trending on social media. His supporters loved him for it, claiming that Coleridge was just telling it like it was when he went on Fox News to complain about "filthy ragheads" and telling viewers that Mexicans were nothing more than "rapists and killers." He was voicing what was in the hearts and minds of Americans everywhere, they said.

Hutchinson had grown to hate them just as much as he hated Coleridge. The president's entire base was little more than insane cult members, and Coleridge was their stomping and screaming foulmouthed revival preacher.

As a member of the president's protective detail, Hutchinson was constantly at war with himself, weighing the importance of his job against the value of his own psyche. His job was to keep Coleridge alive, safe, and secure. If, God forbid, somebody ever tried to assassinate Coleridge, it was Hutchinson's duty to put himself between the president and a bullet. Frankly, if push came to shove, Hutchinson doubted he could do it. Not anymore. Not after four long, hard years of dealing with America's most powerful man-baby.

Instead of arriving early, he'd used the extra time to practice at the shooting range in the basement of the Treasury Building. He was a good shot, and he was intent on keeping his skills honed.

As he approached the Marine officer stationed at the White House entrance, Hutchinson removed his face mask, folded it, and, with a heavy sigh, placed it in the pocket of his black overcoat. Despite the novel coronavirus pandemic and Coleridge's own infection, the White House had adopted a strict no-mask policy. Coleridge viewed this most basic preventive measure against a life-threatening virus to be a sign of weakness. Like all of Coleridge's views, this belief was filtered through his own deranged prism of narcissism and self-loathing, and it had been made policy.

Somehow, despite working in close contact with the man and the members of his staff, Hutchinson had avoided getting sick. He supposed it was always possible he'd caught the illness and had been asymptomatic, but so far, knock on wood, he'd been free of fever, coughing, aches, loss of taste and smell, and the other range of symptoms the coronavirus presented.

As he opened the entrance into the West Wing, a fly landed on his face, buzzing noisily. He swatted at it, annoyed and already in a bad mood. He shook his head as the lone blowfly circled him, and he pushed inside.

What the fuck is a fly doing out here in January?

"Morning, Mike," a soft, feminine voice greeted him as he entered the welcoming warmth of the White House. His mood brightened considerably as Colette fell into rhythm alongside him, and together, they navigated the ground floor hallways of the West Wing.

Colette was one of the most capable, reliable, and forthright agents Hutchinson had ever worked with. She was a skilled marksman and dedicated triathlete who'd competed hard and had a collec-

tion of first place medals to show for it. Those awards were as much a point of pride for her as the Harvard law degree she'd earned as the first woman in her family to go to college. An avid and diverse reader, she was among the smartest people he knew, too. Over the last few months she had also grown into something more than just a highly respected colleague and well-regarded agent.

Although he'd seen her earlier that morning before leaving his apartment, he still flushed warmly at the sight of her. He wished he could kiss her good morning for a second time. "Good morning, Colette," he said, keeping his face impassive and emotionless.

Fraternization between agents was strongly discouraged. As far as Hutchinson knew, nobody was aware of their months-old, off-duty relationship, and both were keen to keep it that way. They were careful to maintain an exceedingly professional relationship within the halls of the White House. The black suits they both wore helped, he thought. It was a bit like playing dress-up, and the clothes and duties gave them roles to fulfill and distract them while on duty. When those suits came off, though…

A sudden rush of heat warmed his cheeks, and he had to tamp down the thoughts of Colette peeling herself out of that black suit and white dress shirt and the way her trousers slithered over her hips and fell down her toned thighs to puddle at her ankles.

As they stepped into the Secret Service's offices, Hutchinson's eyes were immediately drawn to the wall-mounted televisions and the news reports broadcasting live from outside the White House. He stopped to watch as he prepared himself a cup of coffee from the rest station. News anchors outside the White House were hardly something new, and they'd become so much a part of the daily background noise, especially over the last few days following Coleridge's illness, that he barely even registered their presence.

"Earthquake?"

"That's what they're saying. Small and localized. It opened up a sinkhole in the South Lawn."

"Big Enchilada's gonna be pissed if it fucked up his putting green," Hutchinson said, referring to Coleridge by his code name.

"His putting green's covered in snow," Colette reminded him. "He never uses it anyway."

"That's why we're going to Florida this weekend. Again."

The "we" in this context, however, referred only to Hutchinson and the other members of the presidential detail. Colette was assigned to protect the vice president and would be staying in Washington, DC.

She put a soothing hand on his arm then quickly removed it. Coleridge had earned a reputation as an avid golfer as POTUS, using taxpayer money to foot the bill to travel between any one of the number of private resorts he owned across the globe. Although Coleridge routinely bragged at his rallies about sacrificing his $400,000 presidential salary and working for free, his golf trips had cost taxpayers nearly $200 million dollars. A government-spending watchdog group had even established a website to track the number of days Coleridge spent golfing and how much it was costing the American public to subsidize his expensive hobby. The Secret Service had to follow him everywhere he went, which meant that in addition to providing him with security, they also paid him and his family directly in order to stay with him at his resorts. Coleridge got to travel for free, and the Secret Service got billed for room and board, as well as the meals they ate at Coleridge's resorts. Hutchinson had to give Coleridge credit, though—the man was an expert grifter and savvy con artist.

On TV, the news crew aired a video from outside the residence

area of the White House mansion.

"While the world was celebrating the arrival of 2021, it appears the Coleridges were celebrating in their own ways, as well. The following footage was posted early this morning to YouTube—"

Hutchinson ignored the commentary and focused on the imagery. The lights in Coleridge's room went out briefly, then a fresh golden glow slowly relit the interior beyond the gauzy white drapes. A moment later, there was a dazzling eruption of flickering light, and the room briefly glowed red as the candle flames danced. The footage shook, which he attributed to the localized earthquake, then went dark.

"What the hell?" he said, stirring in sugar and powdered creamer.

"Weird, huh?"

This fucking family, he thought.

He took a sip of coffee, savoring the bitter jolt of caffeine. He couldn't wait for Inauguration Day to roll around. If Coleridge refused leave on his own, Hutchinson would be first in line to throw the man out. He relished having the chance to bum-rush that cheap, nickel-and-diming, creepy, racist, old fuck out of the White House for good.

Odds were, though, Coleridge would instead be taking yet another extended vacation at his Florida resort and ignoring the inauguration altogether.

THREE

PRESIDENT COLERIDGE HAD WOKEN UP early enough on New Year's Day to phone in to *Fox & Friends* and assure his viewers that he was in exemplary health and peak physical condition. It was true too. The last few days had put his body through the wringer, but he'd bounced back. He felt absolutely incredible, better than he'd ever felt, maybe. Until he saw Evelyn. Then he felt even better.

Shortly after his impromptu call-in appearance, she strode into the master bedroom where her father lay, his thumbs quickly tapping on his cell phone. She wore a sleek pinstriped pencil skirt that stopped just above mid-thigh and a cream-colored blouse with a pearl necklace around her long, slender throat. As he leered at her breasts, his mind turned to giving her an entirely different sort of pearl necklace.

"How are you feeling, Daddy?"

"I have never been better, baby. I mean that. This is, literally, the best I've ever felt. It's amazing."

She came around to the side of the bed and slipped off her dress jacket, which she tossed over the armrest of the closest chair. Leaning over him, the top of her unbuttoned blouse falling open, Evelyn placed the back of her hand on his forehead. She nodded in approval.

Coleridge couldn't help looking at the display of cleavage dropping toward his face as his daughter took his temperature. She was not wearing a bra, and he wondered if any other undergarments had been forgotten that morning. He smiled up at her, one hand cupping the inside of her knee and slowly sliding upward.

"But you make me feel even better, baby."

She stood straight and tucked a lock of long blond hair behind one ear. Her hip popped to one side as she struck a flirtatious pose, a coy smile playing upon her lips as her hands went to the buttons of her blouse and she undid the rest of them. Then, slowly, she wriggled out of the skirt and stepped out of it. Naked, she straddled her father and leaned in for a deep, long kiss.

His hand groped at her bottom, a finger prodding at her rectum. "Turn around," he growled. "I'm gonna suck a fart out of this ass."

***

Coleridge's schedule for the rest of the day was a blank slate, just as he preferred it. He'd always known being president had to be a cushy job, but even he was genuinely shocked at just how little there actually was to do on a day-to-day basis. Sure, there were the occasional flare-ups, when he had to send in the Navy SEALs to knock on some doors in the Middle East and kill some raghead terrorists or lecture the police on not doing enough to quell the violence running rampant in black neighborhoods—they needed to get tough, crack down, and leave a body count to show they were serious. Or maybe

there was a hurricane, and he had to fly down to some Mexican-infested barrio in Florida or Texas and spend five minutes cheerfully tossing them paper towels with a helping side of thoughts and prayers so they could soak up the water in the filthy little rat nests they called home.

All in all, though, the job was surprisingly dull. He found himself having to invent things to do, issuing sprees of executive orders to undo as many of the prior president's actions as he could. Much of it was little more than showmanship, but as a veteran television star and network ratings goldmine, he knew the importance of flashiness and generating the image he wanted people to see and believe. On one hand, it was pointless theatrics, but on the other hand, it was vitally important. For one thing, it reversed a number of policies the previous president, a black man whom Coleridge was sure hadn't even been born in this country, had put into place. This allowed Coleridge to later rewrite those previously reneged policies into new actions that he could then take credit for.

Much of the work he created for himself was, as he saw it, necessary work to get the country back into healthy, fighting form after so many years of neglect. He saw the way black people treated their neighborhoods, always looting, stealing, and shooting one another, never cutting their lawn, and doing all kinds of drugs. They were lazy and shiftless, and to have one of those people become president infuriated him. He had to fix it. *Had to*. He was the only one who could. He couldn't leave the job until it was done, and there was still so much left to do. Four years wasn't long enough for a great president to be truly effective. Even eight years wasn't enough, not for somebody like Coleridge. He was single-handedly rebuilding the nation in his own image, and that required time. Maybe a lot of time. He wasn't working with a blank slate, after all.

He laughed, pausing in the application of his makeup.

Now there's an idea, he thought. *A blank slate.*

He mused on that notion for a while as he layered on foundation then a deep, rich bronzer, which he smeared over his face and forehead with his fingertips.

When he was done, he returned, naked, to the bedroom. Evelyn was snoring softly atop the rumpled sheets, lying on her belly, her legs spread slightly apart. Her ass quietly whispered as she passed gas in her sleep, and he inhaled deeply, savoring her smell. He detected the odor of a greasy cheeseburger and the slightest tinge of coffee. He thought about waking her up with another rough tumble but decided to let her rest instead. He wasn't sure of the last time he'd ridden her hard enough to leave her so thoroughly exhausted.

Second or third grade, maybe? He shrugged. It wasn't important. Better to let Evelyn get her beauty sleep so she was energized for later. They had a big day ahead of them.

He called his press secretary and told her to arrange a live news conference for 4:00 p.m.

FOUR

HE LOOKS LIKE A FUCKING raccoon, Hutchinson thought upon see-ing Coleridge. The president greeted his Secret Service detail with raised fists, which he pumped in the air as he smiled broadly at them.

Coleridge's makeup was sloppy, and he'd left wide circles around his eyes. While the rest of the man's face was painted an odd, unnatural shade of orange, ghostly white flesh ringed each of his eyes and his pale ears. He looked ridiculous, but what made it even worse was the man honestly thought he looked good like that.

Unbelievable.

Hutchinson followed the older man out of the Oval Office and down the corridors to the Press Briefing Room. He and the other members of the protective detail would stay out of sight in the ad-joining room and behind the blue drapery that provided a backdrop to the speaker's podium. The White House press corps was, obvi-ously, vetted prior to their admission into the West Wing and run through a gauntlet of security as a standard precaution to check for

bombs, firearms, and the like.

He hadn't noted a press conference on the president's incredibly light schedule for the day, but Coleridge favored impromptu, unscripted events and often operated impulsively and erratically. He'd been sick and hadn't been in front of a TV camera in several days. Clearly, he was getting antsy for attention.

Hutchinson noticed Coleridge's family was present in the Briefing Room, which he thought odd. He suspected the presser was an excuse for the president to extoll his superiority over a virus that had killed so many others and ground the nation's economy to a halt, but neither the White House physician nor her staff were present. The VP, whom Coleridge had placed in charge of the emergency pandemic response after firing the White House's actual pandemic-response team shortly after taking office, was also absent. Coleridge had also placed his son Stephen on the emergency response team and often deferred to Stephen's judgements on the crisis over his vice president's. Such judgements had included not only downplaying the severity of the coronavirus but also using federal agents to seize and confiscate shipments of personal protective equipment being delivered to hospitals and agencies in blue states across the country.

Odder still was Coleridge himself. The man had virtually been on life support a week ago. Now he was bounding down the hall and waving his arms like he was about to hop into a wrestling ring. Hutchinson knew the docs at Walter Reed had given him steroids on top of a suite of experimental drugs and oxygen. Still, given how the man had looked when he'd first arrived back at the White House, it struck him that the medical treatments weren't merely effective—they were downright miraculous.

Too bad so many others were denied similar life-saving treatments, Hutchinson thought. He wondered just how different the last year

would have been if they'd had a capable, compassionate, and humane leader at the helm, instead of this raving lunatic.

For lack of anything else better to do and because of the sudden need to use his hands, Hutchinson adjusted his tie and jacket. He took a brief moment to look out at the assembled press, then he went into position in the shadows behind the drapery at the president's back. While masks were verboten among the Coleridges and White House staff and employees, the members of the press corps were all wearing theirs, as they always did when working within The People's House. They were also sensibly spaced apart by the minimum six-foot distance recommended by the CDC. Coleridge had spent the better part of a year undermining such health policies, but wiser heads across the country opted to follow those recommendations regardless.

He checked his watch, which he wore so the face of the timepiece rested on the underside of his wrist. Wearing the watch upside down cut down on glare from the sun, making the watch face easier to read. More importantly, it prevented light from glinting off the glass and giving his position away to others. It was an old trick that had become a habit thanks to his years in Afghanistan with the army. It also helped prevent the watch from getting too banged up, an important consideration nowadays, given how much he'd spent on the latest-generation iWatch.

"Big Enchilada is taking the stage in two minutes," he said, speaking softly into the concealed microphone all USSS agents were issued.

Hutchinson's stomach roiled with the usual butterflies that preceded any of Coleridge's speaking affairs. What was the man going to say, and what kind of reaction would it spark? He remembered one of the president's many rallies a few years back, early in Coleridge's

presidency, when Coleridge went on an anti-free-press rant, calling journalists the "enemy of the people." He'd gotten the attendants so riled up, a handful of them had stormed the press area and attacked the reporters stationed there. One of Coleridge's cultists had used his car key to stab a CNN anchor in the face, punching the piece of metal through her cheek. Fortunately, the local cops working the event were fast-footed and had broken up the mini-riot but not before blood was spilled.

He forced his hands to unclench and relax, but his body was still knotted with nervous energy. He took a deep breath then forced it out slowly. Even despite the president's recent illness, he knew the man was perpetually only a hair's breadth away from flying off the handle at any given moment and letting his anger get the better of him. The press would likely take it easy on him—easier than they should, anyway—but Coleridge would find ways to let himself get baited. He always did. It was but one of the man's many, many weaknesses.

"Okay, it's go time," he said.

Coleridge entered the Press Briefing Room, head held high as he stood before the bullet-resistant lectern situated in front of the White House seal on the wall behind him and flanked on either side by the American flag. His demeanor was proud and strong. He looked powerful, perhaps even more powerful than he'd looked at any time over the last four years. Hutchinson had to admit, it was a hell of a sight compared to the stooping, sickly form they'd all but had to carry aboard *Marine One*.

"I swear, every time I come out here," Coleridge said into the microphone, staring out at the handful of reporters seated before him, "it's like walking into a pit of vipers. You're all just so ready to attack, aren't you? I know it. I know it. But you're not going to be around

here for much longer, are you?"

Coleridge snorted, looking past the assemblage of reporters and to the television cameras and photographers stationed behind them, in front of the large blue video control stations at the rear of the room.

"The recount is not going well for Boozy Barnett. I can tell you that much. It's looking good for us, though. Very, very good. We're not going anywhere." Then Coleridge leaned in very close to the microphone, his head still tilted up toward the cameras as he emphatically announced, "*Nowhere.*"

Hutchinson felt sick watching the display. Seventy-six years old, and the man acted like a spoiled fucking child. His mind reeled at the ridiculousness of it all, and from the President of the United States of America, no less. It was astounding. Worse, he felt completely lost at sea, wondering what the hell Coleridge's endgame was. According to the news reports, the election recounts Coleridge had demanded were only further strengthening Barnett's victory.

So, what the hell is this? He pinched the bridge of his nose, trying to stave off the headache growing behind his eyes. *Just another fucking embarrassment on a global scale for the good ol' US of A.*

"Mr. President?" A pregnant woman in the front row raised her hand, meeting his steely gaze directly. "May Cheng, MSNBC. Following your statement yesterday, upon your return to the White House, a white supremacist group unveiled a new badge for their members that says 'Ready,' within an hour of your telling supporters to, quote, 'Stand By. Be ready.' You've been asked multiple times already, and I am asking again, sir, will you condemn white supremacy?"

Hutchinson watched Coleridge's expression on the overhead monitor. The president's face was calm, but his cold blue eyes were

angry and turbulent. Hutchinson knew that look well. Coleridge was absolutely seething.

"It's always the same with you people, isn't it?"

"What do you mean by 'you people,' Mr. President?"

"You know I had your little *Chinese* virus—"

"Why are you looking at me like that when you call it the 'Chinese virus,' Mr. President?"

"But you slanty-eyed gooks can't kill me, all right? You tried, and you failed. I feel terrific. Better than I ever have before."

The pit in Hutchinson's stomach fell open. Of all the off-the-cuff racist remarks and dog whistles Coleridge had sounded over the years, this was the most outright demeaning he'd ever been. Hutchinson had heard Coleridge use plenty of ethnic slurs behind closed doors before and was constantly astounded by the breadth of the man's dehumanizing vocabulary, but this marked a new low in a presidency constantly defined by how low the bar could be buried.

"Take off your mask," Coleridge said, stepping to the side of the podium. "Take it off, you fucking chink. What are you, afraid? Huh? What've you got to lose? Take it off, I said!"

Cheng stammered, clearly taken as off-guard by the president's hysterics as everyone else in the room. The rest of the press corps were staring wide-eyed between the two, scribbling madly on their notepads.

"Mr. President, this is no way to speak to—"

Coleridge bounded off the small elevated platform of the briefing stage and stormed toward Cheng, screaming obscenities at her.

"Take it off, you fucking slope," he demanded, reaching for her.

Cheng rose from her seat and tried to step away, but Coleridge was surprisingly fast for a man his age and was on top of her in a heartbeat. In the small confines of the Press Briefing Room, a space

barely larger than a decent-sized living room with nearly fifty chairs jammed in, there was nowhere for her to go.

Hutchinson gasped, unable to believe what was happening even as he pushed past the thick curtain and down the stage. Coleridge grabbed Cheng by her crotch and squeezed with one hand, while using the other to tear away her face mask.

The way he leaned in toward her, Hutchinson thought the president was going to kiss her. Or worse. Not that it could get much worse than it already had. The outgoing president had already lobbed a handful of racist slurs on live TV and just sexually assaulted a pregnant reporter.

But get worse it did.

Just as Hutchinson placed a restraining hand on Coleridge's shoulder, the older man's face rocketed forward, his teeth snapping. He bit into Cheng's face, and blood spurted out from between his lips. He shook his head like an angry attack dog, ripping loose a chunk of flesh.

Cheng screamed and fell backward, her hands flying to the wound, shocking the other reporters into action. They leapt to their feet and began pushing their way toward the aisles on either side of the rows of chairs, screaming and shoving at one another as they fumbled for their cell phones. This was going to be one hell of a breaking news story and ratings bonanza.

Hutchinson pulled at the president's shoulder, trying to turn the man around, but Coleridge was immoveable. It was like trying to nudge a building out of the way.

Coleridge's head snapped around toward his Secret Service agent, lips bloodied, and spat the reporter's cheek at his face. Reflexively, Hutchinson let go, and Coleridge pushed him off his feet, flinging him into the first row of vacated chairs. He landed awkwardly, and

painfully, among the upraised seats of the small theater-style chairs.

As he tried to get to his feet, he watched helplessly as the other agents rushed off the stage toward them. Coleridge's family, too, was charging into the fray, all of them fast. Too fast.

Or maybe it was just him. Maybe the world had slowed down, and he was seeing it all through a fog of time dilation.

Melanie, Stephen, David, and Evelyn leaped into the air and landed catlike in the center of the space between the lectern and the seating area before springing forward into the pushing, confused throng of fleeing journalists. Behind the approaching Secret Service, Maddock, Christie, and Diana stood.

The bright lights in the Briefing Room all out went out simultaneously, plunging the area into complete darkness. Then the red emergency lighting came on. A series of noisy metallic shudders echoed through the room as protective barriers fell over the curtained, bulletproof windows. He heard the loud thump of electromagnetic locks engaging on the door separating the Briefing Room from the press corps offices. The locks were fail secure, which meant they would continue to provide security even if the White House lost power and could resist up to a ton of force. The doors themselves were thick, heavy sheets of steel disguised by a wooden finish and lead lined to protect against radiation.

"Priest, get control of this situation now!" A breathless, urgent voice came across his earpiece over the group channel of the presidential protective detail. "We are sealing the room, but have the west entrance open for exfil. Hurry up."

He knew the voice. It was Gregg Lorn in the White House Secret Service Command Center. Obviously, the agents stationed there would have been observing the situation from the room's many overhead cameras, and now they were in the process of enacting emer-

gency security protocols to secure the White House.

He didn't have much time, and he knew the Secret Service wouldn't wait for him long. Hutchinson shoved himself away from the chair and kicked his legs out, trying to maneuver his way back to his feet. One foot had become wedged up in the narrow gap between the seat and chair back, and he fumbled to free himself of it. In the process, he saw the Coleridge family advance on the reporters and heard, too clearly, the screams that followed.

David Coleridge grabbed a silver-haired Fox News reporter by the head and twisted forcefully. The sound of his breaking neck echoed in the small room as David continued to turn the journalist's head until it popped off. A fountain of red showered over him and the other closely packed correspondents.

Stephen grabbed the arm of a writer for the *Washington Post*, tore away the limb, then used it to club a woman from CNN and a nearby *New York Times* newsman. Melanie and Evelyn used fangs and claws, their hands and faces stretching and elongating to accommodate the sudden anatomical changes.

Unable to believe his own eyes, Hutchinson turned toward his fellow agents. He didn't even have time to warn them. The other members of the Coleridge family advanced quickly from behind, their forms hideously mutated by whatever strange affliction coursed through them.

Maddock leapt onto the back of Special Agent in Charge Aaron Priest, the head of the president's protection detail, and rode him to the stage, biting at the man's neck and tearing loose chunks of flesh in a violent spray of gore. Another agent turned to see what this new commotion was, his head swiveling into Diana's waiting talons. Her fingers sank into his eyes, blinding him, then exploded out of the back of his skull. Diana sprang forward, leaping at a third agent's

chest, her arms outstretched. Her clawed hands punched through his pectorals, and they tumbled off the stage, landing near Hutchinson.

As he finally gathered himself up and stood, Hutchinson looked toward the president. Coleridge was hunched over the prone form of May Cheng, his face buried in the cavern of her distended, torn-open belly. He pried something loose from inside her. The wailing cries reached Hutchinson's ears as the president raised the premature infant to his face and bit down on its pale, red-streaked chest. Coleridge's teeth crunched through bone. A fresh gout of bright-red plasma sprayed from between his mouth and the child he suckled upon. The garish noise of the president slurping at the howling baby's innards turned Hutchinson's stomach, and he quickly turned his head aside as his stomach purged itself of its contents.

Hutchinson was outnumbered, his team dead, but the Coleridge family was distracted. He pulled his collapsible ASP baton free and, with a flick of his wrist, expanded it to its full twenty-one-inch length. He ran toward the stage as Christie Coleridge turned toward him with a ravenous, bloodthirsty look in her eyes. He swung the weapon toward her, and the black chrome-plated steel wand smashed into the First Daughter's skull with bone-rattling force, splitting the skin across her forehead. She screamed at him, not out of pain or fright, but in bloodcurdling anger. It wasn't the sound of an injured thirtysomething woman. It was the sound of a ferocious, pissed-off predator. His heart was racing, and he had to tamp down on the rising tide of panic surging through him. The Press Room, the site of an unholy massacre, was awash in blood and gore.

He bounded onto the stage, the hair rising on the back of his neck as he sensed the First Daughter racing at his unprotected rear. He flashed a look over his shoulder, already tensing to recoil away from the swinging claws he knew were waiting for him, but the

woman had moved onto fresher, easier prey. Instead of an attacker, he saw the still-glowing green eye of the news cameras.

The entire world had just watched on live TV as President Coleridge announced his intent to hold on to the White House and then, along with his family, proceeded to murder everyone in the room. Hutchinson was the only person who made it out alive.

88BladesForColeridge
We are standing by and WE ARE READY!!!!
4:15 p.m. - 1 JAN 2021

69MelaniesTwat69
God, @FLOTUS is so fucking hot! I wanna DEVOUR that fucking PUSSY! I wish I could #VoteColeridge a fourth time! LMFAO LOL #AmericanExceptionalism
4:15 p.m. - 1 JAN 2021

NOTABOT!01895457357855926472415978000000000
THAT was the moment Tyler Coleridge truly became President of the Unisted States of America!!!1!!!!11!!!!!
#FuckJournos #FuckThePress #ENemyofthe People
#VoteColeridge #AmericanExceptionalism
4:15 p.m. - 1 JAN 2021

FIVE

HUTCHINSON PUSHED HIS WAY INTO the suite adjoining the Press Briefing Room. Normally, it was in this area, in one of the nearby rooms, where Coleridge would have his makeup fixed or applied, on the rare occasions that he forgot his garish golden fake-tan bronzer, before going in front of the cameras. Normally, it was a relatively calm area.

Today it was bustling with chaos as the makeup artists and president's staffers freaked out and screamed toward the exit in a fit of hysteria. A handful of agents were attempting to get control of the evacuation and get the staffers out of the building in a calmer and more orderly fashion, but it was like trying to herd cats. A few of the panicked office staff even shoved the Secret Service agents out of their way rather than listen and were creating a logjam in the corridor on their frantic run to the exits.

Hutchinson took in the chaotic scene as he pushed the door shut behind him and pressed his back to it, needing a moment to collect his breath. As soon as the door was secured in its frame, the magnetic locks engaged with a solid, metallic *thump* that was beyond reassuring. Just in case, though, he grabbed a nearby chair and wedged it

under the door handle. He had no idea what the fuck was happening to any of them, but he could only hope and pray that the maglocks and steel barriers that had slammed down across the windows would be enough to prevent them from accessing the rest of the White House.

If this had been a normal threat, the security measures would have been more than enough to quell the disturbance. Clearly, though, this was pretty fucking far from normal. If the Coleridges were somehow able to bypass the door locks on the opposite end of the Briefing Room, they would be in the press corps offices. From there, they would have access to the West Colonnade, a route that could take them either back into the residence of the mansion or straight to the Oval Office. If they got through the door Hutchinson was currently pressed against, they had access to everything, including the stairwells that led up to the second floor and down to the ground and underground levels. Hutchinson didn't like either of those options.

Rather than press his way through the crowded stairwell, he shoved his way back into the hallway, retracing his route from the Oval Office earlier. He headed for the stairwell outside the Cabinet Room, which led to the ground floor and terminated directly outside the Secret Service Command Center entrance. Rushing down the steps, he radioed Colette. A sudden worry nagged at him that she wouldn't—or couldn't—answer, and he had to force that dark thought aside.

"Colette, what's your status?"

"Securing the cabinet and vice president," she said. "We are en route to the Hole."

"Good," he said. He let out a relieved sigh, grateful to hear her voice, and thankful she was hustling to get her team and protectee to

safety. The Hole was the unofficial name for the underground emergency bunker beneath the White House. He wondered how much she knew about what was happening and if the SSCC had relayed any specifics to the other members of the White House security. "Get there and stay there. Keep them safe. And good luck."

His feet hit the bottom step, and he rounded the staircase heading toward the exit. His cellular phone rang as he burst into the hallway leading to the offices of the Secret Service. It was a phone number he recognized but one that rarely had need to contact him directly.

"This is Hutchinson," he said.

"What in the fucking name of God's green earth is happening over there?" a stern and deeply troubled voice shouted into his ear.

"Director Barnes, I honestly don't even know where to begin. The Coleridge family... Sir, they've lost it. President Coleridge snapped and attacked a reporter. His family joined in and eliminated nearly all of the agents assigned to protect them."

"I know what happened, goddamn it. What I need to know is: *What. The. Fuck. Happened? Why* did this happen?"

"Sir, I don't know."

Hutchinson's heart raced. He wondered if this was what an impending heart attack felt like. Hearing noises of frustration and the shuffling of paperwork in the background, Hutchinson realized additional people were on the line with the director. Confirming that thought, another voice joined in.

"Agent, this is Deputy Director Crouch. I'm here with Director Barnes and Chief Operating Officer Gavin. Is there any reason to suspect that President Coleridge's actions are the result of terrorism? Perhaps a chemical assault, a nerve agent, something of the like?"

As Deputy Director, Crouch was the man responsible for over-

seeing the daily operations of the Office of Protective Operations, Strategic Intelligence and Information, and Mission Support, among other elements within the Secret Service.

"I do not believe so, sir. Each member of the press corps and the Press Briefing Room itself were inspected prior to President Coleridge taking the stage. I have no reason, at this time, to conclude that today's events were a product of outside forces."

"So you're saying this is the result of internal forces? One of our own?"

"No, sir, I am not suggesting that at this time. Simply put, I have no information on the hows and whys of any of this."

Gavin spoke up next, her voice silky smooth. "So what you are saying, or perhaps not saying, Agent Hutchinson, is what? POTUS just had a psychotic break on live television?"

"Ma'am, with all due respect, I do not see an alternative. No other parties in that room were affected by a pathogen, biological, chemical, or otherwise. The Coleridges were the only ones who launched an attack on those gathered."

"You attacked the First Daughter!" Barnes said.

"I did, sir. Based on their behaviors, I judged the First Daughter and every other member of the Coleridge family in that room to be a clear and immediate threat to my life, and I responded with the force I felt was appropriate."

Hutchinson swallowed a jagged lump caught in his throat. He was supposed to protect the president and his family. Instead, he'd attacked one of them and watched helplessly as they, quite literally, tore apart everyone in that room. He'd been powerless to stop them.

There was silence on the other end of the line. He suspected the gathered leadership of the Secret Service, if they were all together in the United States Secret Service Headquarters building half a mile

away, took a moment to exchange looks as they weighed the scant information they'd just been provided.

Slowly, all the things that were being left unsaid began to dawn on Hutchinson. He noticed, then, how the event was being referred to by his superiors and how that green camera light had glowed. "How contained is this?"

Crouch sighed deeply, while Barnes swore in the background. The Deputy Director said, "We were able to jam the transmitting signal from the cameras and cell phones and commandeer the live broadcast feeds from the TV news cameras inside the Briefing Room. As far as the outside world knows, all Coleridge did was get in a reporter's face and hurl insults at her. Some of the networks, like ABC and NBC, cut away to their anchors before he even left the stage. Once it became clear that the situation was, let's say, untenable, we jammed it. We—that is, those of us in the command level—were able to monitor the situation as it evolved. Nothing is getting in or out of the White House."

Hutchinson swore softly to himself. He could already smell the cover-up coming.

"We're thinking," Gavin said, "that perhaps it was an extreme neurological reaction to the experimental medications the president was given to treat his infection. We're drafting a statement now for Dr. Roth and the senior officials at Walter Reed."

"Excuse me for saying so, ma'am, but I don't know if that's the appropriate way to describe this situation."

"What would you have us say?" Barnes said. "Huh? That the President of the United fucking States just ate a goddamned baby? That your goddamn motherfucking protectees just fucking straight-up slaughtered the fucking press corps and the entire protective detail of highly trained United States fucking Secret Service agents? Is

that the appropriate way to describe this motherfucking clusterfuck of a goddamned fucking *situation*, Agent Hutchinson?"

Hutchinson could picture Barnes's bright-red, fuming face. If they were in a cartoon, steam would be shooting out of the director's ears and nostrils, with plumes of jetting smoke accompanied by a high-pitched train whistle noise, and the top of his head would explode from the pressure of a booming mushroom cloud.

Chastised, Hutchinson answered softly, "No. No, sir. I apologize if I was out of line."

"What are things like on the ground?" Crouch said.

"The president's cabinet and the vice president are currently en route to the bunker. The White House is locked down and secure."

"Good. I want this contained. Do you understand me? Get this shitshow resolved. *Now.*"

"Yes, sir. I understand."

"The president and his family are not—I repeat, *not*—to leave the White House grounds. We need them contained." There was a pause as Crouch weighed his next words, and when he spoke next, there was a weight of tragedy to his voice as he succumbed to the reality of the situation. "Alive, if possible."

"Yes, sir."

"Barnes is coordinating with Homeland to provide additional support, if needed, but we're keeping this quiet. In the meantime, I suppose this makes you Special Agent in Charge. Congratulations, Hutchinson. Get it done. You hear me?"

The line went dead. It took a moment for Crouch's final words to sink in. Intellectually, he knew SAC Priest was dead—he'd seen the man damn near decapitated by an eleven-year-old—but only now was the weight of that murder catching up to him.

He stopped, his chin sinking to his chest as he pressed his fore-

head to the wall. His short reverie was broken by his phone ringing a second time.

***

Hutchinson looked down at his phone. He recognized this number as well, and it pained him to send the call to voicemail. He so desperately wanted to talk to his son. *It could be the last time*, a defeated voice said inside him.

But now was not the time for that. He had a lot of work to do first, and the pressure of being embroiled in the middle of an entirely unprecedented national emergency consumed him.

With communications into and out of the White House blocked, regular civilian lines wouldn't function. Right now, he knew, there were tourists milling about Washington, DC, their cell phones no longer sending or receiving calls and unable to find any kind of a signal. The White House was equipped with military-grade jamming technology that interfered with the frequencies and satellite transmissions of civilian radios and phones.

Hutchinson and his fellow Secret Service agents were hardly civilians, and their government-issued cell phones, radios, and communications equipment broadcast on secure, encrypted, government frequencies or through government satellites.

He looked down at the phone as its notifications screen darkened and, a moment later, relit with a voicemail alert from his kid. He banged his forehead against the wall, gently at first, then harder a second time, and a third, until tears stung his eyes.

"Goddamn it," he said softly, to himself, the flat side of his fist striking the wall beside his head.

Hutchinson hated to admit that keeping information on the

current crisis in the White House contained was likely easier now than it might have been under past presidencies. The election of Coleridge had prompted a significant number of upgrades to security within the building itself and on the surrounding property. The inauguration had been met with widespread protests, and the recent Black Lives Matter marches outside the White House had led to the installation of extra layers of fencing all around the perimeter, barricades in the street, and the redirection of both pedestrian and vehicular traffic around 1600 Pennsylvania Avenue. A far cry from previous administrations, the People's House now operated more like a prison than the head of a democratic government. It was damn near impossible to penetrate the exterior of the perimeter and was just as difficult to escape unnoticed by the layered webs of surveillance and protection measures.

This wasn't how things were supposed to be, though. If he were being entirely honest with himself, nothing involving the Coleridge administration was how things were supposed to be, but he still had a job to do.

When he was a kid, his parents had brought him to DC on vacation one summer, during the early years of the first Bush administration. They'd just about been able to walk in off the sidewalk to take part in the daily White House tours. Now, visitors needed to contact their Congressional reps and give six months' advance notice of their intent to tour the building so background screenings and security checks could be conducted. After 9/11, everything had changed, but even that was minor compared to the turmoil Coleridge had inflicted upon the Union. His bungling of the coronavirus pandemic had left an ever-increasing death toll that far exceeded those caused by the 9/11 terrorist attack that had sparked so much national panic, led the creation of the Department of Homeland Security, and em-

broiled the United States in a war that was nearing its second decade. With over three hundred thousand dead, Coleridge was still taking to the television to blame it on a liberal hoax and call it fake news. With his handling of national and global politics, Coleridge's presidency had only served to paint an even bigger target on the White House.

Still, Hutchinson fondly recalled slowly wandering the White House as a kid, touring the limited number of rooms that were open to the public, and watching the silent, serious sentinels dressed in black suits standing watch on the grounds and inside the house. That was when he'd known, at seven or eight years old, that he wanted to work the presidential protection detail.

His time in the army after 9/11 and then, after his years at Rutgers, as a state investigator working fraud cases for the New York Attorney General's Office, had been a roadmap toward pursuing his dreams of becoming a United States Secret Service agent. While he personally found the entire Coleridge family loathsome and among the pettiest human beings he had ever had the displeasure of meeting—and he'd met plenty of awful, petulant people over his forty-two years—he knew that in the grand scheme of things they amounted to very little in the totality of the history of the United States. They were just a minor bump in the road. Coleridge might be the least deserving man in history to possess the title Commander-in-Chief, but the office itself, the institution of the presidency, its legacy and its future, was an ideal that Hutchinson firmly believed in, and it was far more important than any one single man or woman.

It was his duty to ensure the safety of the president. And he would continue to do that for as long as it was an option. Coleridge and his family had to be subdued and taken into custody for their own sake.

But still, the questions and concerns nagged at him. *What if this was a terrorist attack? What if, heaven forbid, it was something worse?*

He didn't have any answers. But he did have a job to do. He took a deep breath, adjusted his jacket and tie, and entered the Command Center.

***

The Command Center was abuzz with activity as bodies moved back and forth and voices competed for attention. Although it had the air of unbridled chaos, Hutchinson knew these agents were guided by professionalism and years upon years of training. Even if there was an underlying panic, a sort of nervous energy rippling through the air, it was a controlled chaos.

As the magnetic lock released and he pushed through the door, all eyes turned toward him. Hutchinson headed directly to the heart of the Command Center—the Hive—and its long wall of monitors broadcasting feeds from hundreds of closed-circuit surveillance cameras within the White House and along the exterior grounds. Nearby, other agents controlled the fleet of aerial drones that constantly surveilled the White House grounds. Others still monitored the system of infrared sensors they relied on to detect land-based, aerial, or subterranean intrusions around the perimeter of the White House.

Hutchinson went directly to Gregg Lorn, head of the Command Center. They exchanged curt nods and a quick handshake in the glow of the room's TVs.

"What's the status of the Coleridges?"

"We have them confined to the Press Briefing Room. Doors and windows are holding."

Lorn pointed at the series of feeds coming from the various cam-

eras within the Briefing Room, including the hijacked news camera broadcasts. The grisly sight was enough to turn Hutchinson's stomach.

President Coleridge's face and hair were smeared with blood and grease from that reporter and her baby. His belly was distended, pushing against the constraining buttons of his stained, once-white dress shirt. He was kneeling in the gore of his meal, the woman's intestines draped across his slick lap. Coleridge raised his head, a chunk of meat in hand, and looked toward one of the broadcast cameras. He let out a loud, resounding belch. The agent charged with observing those feeds had to turn his head and look away, his cheeks bulging as he fought to swallow down his rising sickness.

On another monitor, one of the angled overheads in the northeast corner of the room, looked down upon Evelyn Coleridge. She was straddling the still body of Agent Heather Anderton, her head pressed down against the woman's face, mouth to eye. For a moment, Hutchinson wondered if Evelyn was kissing the dead woman, but then the awful truth became apparent. Evelyn wasn't kissing Heather—she was sucking the woman's eyeball out of her skull. She looked toward the camera, Heather's eye pinched between her teeth, lips smiling around it, as the optic nerve dangled across her chin. She bit down, and a gush of white watery fluid dripped from her mouth. She swallowed then went to work on the second eye. The other members of the president's family were similarly placated as they feasted upon the dead.

Hutchinson had never seen so much unbridled carnage in his entire life. "Gas the room," he said. "Get me Howett in ERT and have medical on standby."

Lorn nodded smartly and executed the command.

Hutchinson watched as smoke flooded out of the overhead vents

in the briefing room, blanketing the room in a misty haze. The gas was a sweet-smelling inhalational anesthetic known as sevoflurane. While it was most commonly used in hospitals and veterinary clinics to put patients to sleep prior to surgery, it was also a layer of protection employed in the security and defense of the White House. If the building were ever breached by hostile forces, all of the building's rooms would be locked down and the contained intruders would be gassed into submission. Hutchinson had never thought he would see the day they had to use it on the First Family.

Lorn handed over a phone. "Howett."

"It's Hutchinson," Mike said. "You're aware of the situation in here? Good. Get your team prepped for nonlethal infil and extraction of the Press Briefing Room. The room is in lockdown, and sevoflurane has been administered."

"Roger," Howett said, and the line went dead.

Within minutes, they watched as a contingent of the Emergency Response Team approached the West Wing. All the members of the ERT were clad in black combat uniforms, their faces covered by gas masks to prevent inhalation of the fast-acting anesthetic that would rapidly shut down their central nervous systems.

Lorn communicated with the team, navigating them through the perimeter and unsealing the electromagnetic locks room by room. Weapons raised and ready, they quickly breached the Palm Room and fanned out.

"Clear," said the agents as they swiftly checked the corners of the Palm Room for threats and deemed the area free of hostiles. Then they approached the press corps offices, and again, Lorn disengaged the magnetic locks, allowing them entry.

The ERT team swept through the collection of offices and cubicles that made up the press corps room and verified the work areas

were empty.

"Clear!"

They regrouped at the opposite end of the room, forming a half circle around the door leading directly into the Press Briefing Room.

Lorn provided them with an update on the Coleridge's status. "The First Family appears to be unconscious. You are clear to approach, but use caution."

The locks disengaged, and Howett led his team into the heart of the massacre.

Through his earpiece, Hutchinson could hear the squelching of the ERT's boots as they stepped onto the sodden carpeting. That noise was quickly drowned out by gunfire and screaming.

SIX

JONATHAN HOWETT WAS THE FIRST man into the Press Briefing Room. As soon as heard the metallic *chunk!* of the mag locks releasing, he was pushing through the door. His feet sank into the plush carpeting, the wetness creating a suction against the bottom of his combat boots.

He was grateful for the gas mask, which filtered out the stench of the room. He'd been in similar rooms in the past when he was with Force Recon in Kandahar, and his sense memory was more than ready to fill in the blanks for him. His time in the Sandbox came back to him, the cool underground caverns filled with the remains of tortured, butchered servicemen and abducted contractors in Afghanistan or Americans volunteering their medical skills to the wounded civilians. He recalled, too easily, the burning stink of marines blown apart by IEDs.

The Press Briefing Room looked like a twisted amalgamation of both those awful scenarios, its once-pristine white walls messily smeared red. The small size of the room itself and the number of

dead inside somehow made it all the worse. The room was an abattoir.

Behind him, the three other shooters of his Emergency Response Team fanned out to clear the room, using a tactic known as "slicing the pie." The squad members cleared the door and seeped across the room, moving over the bodies as they spread into the narrow aisles on either side of the seating, and the small spaces at the front and back of the room, between the lectern and the video control stations. Their eyes and guns moved in a fast arc as they sought out any threats in the room. Their feet moved wetly across the gore-soaked Berber carpeting as they stomped through putrescent puddles of human filth.

"Briefing Room is clear," Howett said into his communications mic. "The First Family appears to be unconscious. Moving in to secure the packages."

"Roger that," Hutchinson said, his voice small and tinny in Howett's earpiece.

Howett stepped around a discarded limb—somebody's arm—and over the broken-open torso of a different victim who still possessed all their arms and legs. He looked down briefly, not wanting to accidentally step into the open cavity of the man's chest. Splintered ribs jutted out at crazily twisted angles. The organs beneath were pulped into lumpy pieces of purple tissue.

"Christ," he muttered.

President Coleridge was on his side, caked in gore, near the stage, where he'd been speaking only a short time ago. It almost—but only *almost*—reminded Howett of his nephew's first birthday. Ty had been so eager to taste his first-ever piece of cake that he'd dove into the thing—*literally!*—face-first. When he'd resurfaced for air seconds later, his mouth and nostrils were filled with yellow cake, and choco-

late frosting covered every square inch of bare skin and was all up in his hair. Fistfuls of the dessert had clumped around his fingers and smeared up to his elbows. That was what POTUS looked like; only he wasn't smeared in cake. He was slathered in blood and loose flecks of skin and organ meat.

"Jesus Christ," Howett said again. "Wrap them up. Let's hustle."

His stomach had curled into a tight fist, and he wanted to get this over with. The sooner they could secure the president and his family, the sooner he could turn them over to the medical team waiting with gurneys in the press corps office.

The amount of sevoflurane the First Family had inhaled should have been enough to keep them sedated for hours, giving the ERT plenty of time to secure the entire First Family and transport them to the White House Medical Unit, where they could be confined and treated. The WHMU could treat any medical emergency and trauma that occurred within the White House and was essentially a private urgent care center for the president, staffed by twenty-four physicians, medics, and nurses trained to provide emergency care, resuscitation, and trauma care. If an urgent health matter arose, emergency surgery could even be performed, and the medical team could provide care to the patient until they could be safely transported to a hospital.

Given the sheer insanity of what had transpired in the Briefing Room, Howett loathed the idea of transporting the Coleridges off White House grounds. In the WHMU, they would be confined, examined, and tested until it was clear none of them posed any further threat to the safety of others… or could at least be reasonably contained. He had no idea what the hell had caused all this, but he was damn sure there wasn't going to be a repeat of this incident.

Howett gently rolled the president onto his stomach so he could

loop plastic zip ties around the man's wrists and cuff him behind his back. He also bound the president's ankles as an added precaution. He wished he had one of those Hannibal Lecter masks to fit over the man's face. When he was finished, he made sure the man's breathing was not obstructed and that the president wasn't drowning in all the blood he'd spilled.

"How we doing?" he asked his team.

He was met with a variety of positive replies. Everyone was working quickly and diligently to constrain Coleridge's wife and children. Everything was proceeding as normal as it possibly could in this shit-fucked hellscape of a room. The Briefing Room looked like a slaughterhouse.

And then it sounded like one too.

The sound of plastic snapping apart drew Howett's attention in time to see Diana, Coleridge's eldest daughter, flex her freed hands and twist her torso, her legs kicking up at the nearest agent's face. She caught him between her calves, her ankles crossing behind his head, and dragged him down on top of her. Then she grabbed either side of his head and pulled, decapitating him as easily as if she'd just flicked off the head of a dandelion with her thumb. She kicked upward again, pushing against the floor with her hands, and somersaulted into the air, landing on her feet. She sent a palm strike into a second agent, his face caving inward beneath the inhuman blow.

The noise of more plastic restraints breaking filled the air, softer than the sound of breaking bones. One by one, each zip tie snapped apart, and the Coleridges rose.

"I need backup!" Howett screamed into his headset. "I need backup right now! Seal this room!"

Howett raised his 5.56mm Knight's Armament Company SR-16 CQB rifle and opened fire. He and his men were equipped with

rubber-bullet loadouts, and while the ammunition was considered nonlethal, it could still do a hell of a lot of damage. Especially at such close range.

Diana's body jittered backward as a three-round burst stitched its way up and across her chest. Her gaze fell upon Howett, and a wicked smile chilled him to the bone. Then she laughed at him.

What the fuck are they on?

He fired again, a single shot to her head. The rubber bullet crashed into her skull, just above her eye. Her eyebrow split open, wide and nasty, spiling a thick curtain of blood down her face.

Behind her, another member of the ERT, Enriquez, opened fire as Christie and Evelyn approached him. Like Diana, both women were unfazed by the barrage of bullets slamming into their torsos, even as the enormous foot pounds of velocity struck them squarely in the chest and knocked them back a step or two.

Evelyn's lips peeled apart as she roared, leaping into the hair, and slammed Enriquez to the ground. They landed hard, tacky droplets of plasma splashing around them as they hit the carpet. Evelyn was quicker to recover. She did not make Enriquez's death a noble one.

Howett realized then that he was alone now. He looked past Christie, at the rapidly closing door. Diana's head followed his eyes toward the diminishing entryway leading into the press corps offices.

Lorn in the Command Center was on top of his game, at least, and the door was already nearly closed. As soon as Diana had risen from her slumber, Howett had noted the door beginning to swing shut. Although it felt much, much longer, the Coleridge women had taken only a few seconds to slaughter his entire team after awakening.

Diana was the closest one to the door, and she was impossibly fast.

She moved like lightning, her hand reaching into the rapidly shrinking gap of the remotely controlled door. The steel door slammed shut on her fingers, and she roared in pain and fury. As the largest woman in the Coleridge family, she had enough meat on her thick hand to keep the door from sealing completely shut, even if only just barely.

But just barely was good enough.

Howett watched the impossible happen. Diana pushed the door back open, working her good hand into the small gap she'd made, her teeth gritted against the exertion. She put her all into fighting against the automatic hydraulics of the door and its mechanized systems, straining against all the tons of pressure that were supposed to keep it shut and sealed. Then Christie and Evelyn were working their smaller, flatter hands into the gap, helping to pull.

The women had the door open again before Howett could even retrain his weapon on Diana, and they were pulling it off its hinges. Sparks of electricity shot out from between the door and the doorjamb as live circuits were torn apart and destroyed.

He brought his rifle up and aimed at her back, muttering, "Oh shit, oh shit, oh shit," over and over.

Where the fuck is that backup?

Diana smirked at him. Her hand and fingers looked like a banana that had just been stepped on. The smashed digits hung loosely from thin strings of flesh, dangling and dancing in the air. He watched them sway, mesmerized, until one finally snapped loose and plopped against the carpet. Head tilted to the side, she laughed, her hips swaying, as she plucked the other pulped and useless fingers off her hand, as if she were doing nothing more than pulling grapes from the stem.

Just as Howett's finger began to pull against the trigger, pain

exploded in the back of his knee, and his leg buckled. Something grabbed at the back of his vest, and he was pulled off his feet, down onto the carpet, his gun firing uselessly at the ceiling.

The last thing he saw was President Coleridge's clacking teeth, thick strands of red drool hanging from the man's cracked lips, and the leering faces of his eldest two sons crowding in at the edge of his darkening vision.

<u>SEVEN</u>

V ICE PRESIDENT GRAHAM NEALY AND the twenty-two other members of the cabinet were quickly herded out of the Cabinet Room by a contingent of Secret Service agents. Nealy tried to press them for details but was stonewalled by the head of his protective detail, Colette Bridges, who promised him he would be filled in as soon as he was secure.

"Are we under attack?"

Rather than answer, the haughty black woman put a hand on the small of his back, encouraging him to move faster as he was briskly guided through the corridor. They rushed past the Oval Office and the Roosevelt Room and into the emergency freight elevator, whose doors were standing open and waiting for them.

The cabinet had been assembled to discuss the transition between the forty-fifth and forty-sixth presidents. Because of his health, Coleridge wasn't expected to attend, and in Nealy's judgement, that was most certainly a good thing. Coleridge had a bad habit of hijacking the meetings to rant and rave about his favored ill topics of the

day. The last thing Nealy wanted was to listen to more of Coleridge's boisterous delusions about liberal Hollywood celebrities, QAnon conspiracy theories, or, as was most common in the weeks since the election, screeds against his allies within the GOP and the various judges who he believed had helped to rig the election against him.

Most recently, Coleridge had been on the attack against two of his own cabinet members, Attorney General George Racine and Secretary of State John Bonny. The president blamed both men equally for failing to implicate his presidential rival, Marcus Barnett, in various scandals and wrongdoing. Even before Barnett had secured his party's nomination as a presidential candidate, Coleridge had generated a storm of controversy around Barnett. During his rallies and press briefings, Coleridge had accused him of not only meddling with the affairs of foreign governments but also of being a pedophile and sex slave trader. Coleridge's claims were utterly unfounded and baseless, and he considered Racine's and Bonny's inability to unearth supporting evidence to be a personal slight against himself, one that was tantamount to treason. More than once over the last few weeks, Coleridge had made asides about firing squads and promised that things were going to change during his second term.

Considering Coleridge's attacks on his own FBI and CIA directors, as well as the CDC and even his own health experts, it had come as little surprise to any of the cabinet members when the president turned on them too.

Privately, Nealy was greatly anticipating Barnett's inauguration. The sooner Coleridge was out of office, the better. Nealy had played the part of lap dog for the president well over the last four years, but it had been a bitter pill to swallow. Coleridge's antics and behaviors did not jibe with how Nealy believed a man should behave, but he'd held his tongue. The only people he'd shared his concerns with were

his wife and his priest, whom he sought out for the salvation of his soul every Sunday morning during confession.

"Are we under attack?" he asked again.

Bridges took a deep breath, a strange expression crossing her face. Seeing her look so discomposed troubled him, and it was as plain as day that she was calculating the best ways to deliver the news.

She opened her mouth and, a moment later, said, "Yes, sir. We are. You'll be fully debriefed once we reach the Hole and have it secured."

The Hole. He'd never liked that name for the White House's underground bunker. To him, it sounded dirty and sexually perverse. His face flushed at the mere mention of the word. His thoughts drifted to his wife, whom he called Mother, as he lay facedown in bed, naked and spread-eagle, his wrists and ankles tightly bound by rope to the head and foot boards of their bed. Mother, dressed in glossy black leather and a harness fitted with a thick black dildo strapped around her waist, grabbed him by the back of his head as she whispered in his ear, her hot breath ruffling his gray hair. "I'm going to stick this big black dick in your hole, you little bitch." Her hand made wet noises as she stroked the well-lubricated artificial cock, and he begged her to fill his asshole and fuck him raw.

He put a finger between his neck and collar, stretching the fabric. The elevator felt small and hot, trapped as he was between so many bodies.

"Mo—" he began then stopped. "My wife? Is she safe?"

"Agents are attending to her now, and she is being moved to shelter," Bridges said then turned to the rest of the cabinet. "All of your families will be safe."

Nealy's ears popped under the increasing pressure of their rapid descent. The Hole was a self-contained facility four thousand feet

underground, meant to provide long-term shelter in case of a terrorist attack or nuclear emergency. It had been built entirely in secret—which was no small feat, considering the amount of planning, excavation, and construction required—and, like the White House itself, was outfitted with the latest state-of-the-art technologies.

The last time Nealy had been in the Deep Underground Command Center, a more appropriate name than the Hole in his estimation, was in June. The administration had played it off as little more than a routine check of the facility and a test of their emergency preparedness, but the truth of the matter was that they had been afraid the White House would come under assault.

In addition to grappling with a global pandemic, Coleridge had also had to deal with wildfires that had raged across much of the western seaboard from Oregon to California and massive nationwide protests sparked by police violence against Black Americans. The last year had been an utter shitstorm of one bad break after another for the Coleridge administration, made all the worse by Coleridge himself.

The man lacked any sort of tact and was completely blinded to any suffering outside of his own. His utter lack of empathy was inversely proportional to his oversized ego and narcissism. At a time when he could have exhibited some sense of compassion for a divided and wounded America, he had instead deployed US troops to various cities, including Washington, DC. Then, he had ordered those troops outside the White House to clear out the protestors, a peaceful, worshipful group who believed Black Lives Mattered and who were led by priests from the neighboring house of worship known as "The Church of the Presidents," by shooting tear gas and rubber bullets into the crowd. Coleridge then posed at the church for a photo op, where he held a Bible upside down beside his grinning mug and

encouraged people to vote for him on November third.

Both the military and Secret Service worried that, as protests continued to grow across the country and increased dramatically in size outside the White House, in response to Coleridge's supposed show of strength, the People's House would become a target. Protestors had begun toppling statues of Confederate leaders and other landmarks that they said celebrated America's racist past, like Christopher Columbus statues in Detroit, Chicago, New York City, and dozens of other cities. They feared it was only a matter of time that, fueled by Coleridge's own racist outbursts, the White House would come under assault as well.

Nealy wondered if that were it, then. Had the president finally said something so repugnant, so repulsive, that the people had finally said enough was enough? Had he finally crossed a line so stark that America simply wasn't willing to wait even just a few more weeks to be rid of the contemptible, filthy little man?

The elevator eased to a stop, jolting softly as it braked to a halt. When the doors parted, the first thing he saw were two uniformed soldiers standing at attention to greet him and the cabinet. The DUCC was staffed 24/7 by members of the White House Military Office, which itself was comprised of military aides and soldiers from all five branches of the armed forces.

The two soldiers led Nealy to one of the nearby golf carts. There were a number of electronic carts parked there, and once the vice president and his protective detail were situated, the cabinet members and their accompanying agents filled out the rest. They drove together down a two-mile long shaft that was barely wider than two of the carts put side by side. Several minutes later they arrived at a massive vaulted entrance with armed guards, not unlike those that had met the cabinet at the elevator, positioned on either side of the

enormous steel door.

Nealy approached the door and rested his hand against a digital hand scanner, while he stared into the retinal reader positioned at eye level. His identify confirmed, WHMO's most-senior officer stepped forward and initiated a similar protocol to finalize the vice president's access sequence and confirm the cabinet's entry into the Command Center beyond.

Inside, it was like something out of one of the newer *Star Trek* shows, all bright and flashy and incredibly high-tech. A sea of camouflaged bodies bustled around the room, wearing electronic headsets and carrying iPads in rugged protective cases, as they relayed and received updates to and from the majors up above. Banks of monitors streamed feeds from the various internal and external security cameras, aerial drones, and satellite surveillance of the White House, while others were tuned to each of the nation's major cable news network broadcasts.

"Major Henderson, USAF," a tall, wide, beefy man approached the vice president with his hand extended. They shook, and Nealy exchanged pleasantries, feeling entirely out of his element here.

His head was spinning with the potential worst-case scenarios that had brought him here. He looked around for Coleridge, but didn't see the man anywhere, except on two of the cable news feeds, one of which had a prominent banner above its news chyron proclaiming President Slurs Reporter.

Nealy shook his head, wondering if all this was a result of today's impromptu press briefing.

What the hell has that idiot done now? He spent a moment delivering a silent prayer as he, the cabinet, and their protective details followed Henderson and his aides down a shiny, tiled corridor to a large conference room. The room was filled by a massive wooden

table and leather chairs and a host of currently darkened monitors along one entire wall. Glasses of water and several pitchers had been positioned at each seat for the men and women of the cabinet.

Nealy took a seat at the head of the table opposite, so that his back was against the wall and he could see whoever came and left the room. The rest of the cabinet settled into their seats as well.

"Now," Nealy said, "will somebody please tell me what the heck is going on here?"

**

AG George Racine watched as Nealy's face blanched. On the television, the thirty-minute-old recording of Coleridge's press briefing was playing. Nealy had grown increasingly discomfited by Coleridge's behavior as the full immensity of the situation settled on his shoulders. Not at what President Coleridge had said to that Asian reporter—no, sadly, he knew Nealy was used to such profane, racist outbursts from the man, although Coleridge usually at least had the decency to air only the worst of his vitriol behind closed doors and in private, instead of shouting them live on air. So, in that regard, it wasn't Coleridge's behavior behind the podium that troubled Nealy so deeply. It was what came after. It was what the cameras had captured for their private consumption and which could never—*never!*—be released to the media.

"You're positive they don't have this?" he asked, referring to the various news outlets the White House press corps reported for.

"This absolutely cannot get out," Nealy said. "My God, if this"— he waved his hand at the nearby television screen—"*this* got onto the five o'clock news... I can't even begin to imagine... If CNN got this... I mean..."

Racine rubbed his face with both hands, supremely exhausted. The adrenaline that had coursed through him during the flight underground had been spent, and all it had left behind was severe tiredness. The panic he somehow hadn't felt then keenly made its presence felt now.

"Mr. Vice President," the Attorney General said into the shocked, quiet air, "I believe it's time to begin the transfer of power."

"What do you mean, George?" This from Coleridge's Chief of Staff, Robert Connolly.

Racine took off his glasses and rubbed at the corner of his eyes. Everybody knew exactly where Connolly's loyalties lay, and it wasn't with the Office of the Presidency or the United States of America. It was with Coleridge himself, completely and resolutely.

"Obviously, President Coleridge is no longer capable of executing his oath to the office and to the American people," Secretary of State John Bonny said, as delicately as he could.

"I mean, he looks pretty capable, don't you think?" Connolly said, a delighted smirk on his face. "The way he tore those bastards apart?"

"This isn't the time for jokes, goddamn it," Racine said, throwing his glasses down on the table. They skittered to the opposite end and dangled on the edge briefly before falling. He turned to Nealy and said, "Apologies, sir."

Racine knew how devout Nealy was and how much the VP disliked hearing his Lord's name taken in vain. Racine considered himself a religious man as well, and Nealy's own strength of faith made him want to be a better, more pious man. Coleridge and Nealy... now there was an odd couple. *Christ.*

As gross as Connolly's remarks had been, Racine knew the man's viewpoint represented a larger issue they would have to face. It was

notoriously difficult to remove a sitting president from office, and even if they declared this an event worthy of Coleridge's removal by the Twenty-Fifth Amendment—and in Racine's eyes, how could they not? As much as Hutchinson was loath to admit it, Coleridge's allies would only be further emboldened by the man's latest display of gratuitous excess. They would find ways to contort themselves into previously unheard-of positions to support Coleridge's murdering of a roomful of reporters, casting him as some sort of savior of the Republic, a new American Messiah. They'd spend Sunday morning on *Meet the Press* trying to convince people that Coleridge's cannibalism, his eating of a fucking unborn baby in front of news cameras, was somehow a strength, a virtue, a rugged go-get-'em, take-the-bull by the horns display that was uniquely Coleridge.

"We got any Tums?" Racine asked, turning to his aide with a hand out.

If they enacted the Twenty-Fifth Amendment, it would be up to Congress to approve the transfer of power within twenty-one days. If something similar had happened under any other administration, Racine would have thought the transition to be a no-brainer, a no-questions-asked scenario. Under Coleridge, though, the proposition was murkier. To further complicate matters, the Senate Majority Leader might do his level best to disrupt the transfer as a matter of theater and work to prevent the Speaker of the House, a Democrat, from assuming the role of vice president. With Inauguration Day only a short time away, Racine could easily see the House and the Senate waging war with each other in an effort to stall an official transfer of power.

Racine felt the weight of culpability on his own shoulders too. With less than twenty days until the Inauguration, impeachment was out of the question. Coleridge had already been impeached once,

and Racine had argued then, with the support of House Republicans behind him, that the sitting president could not be prosecuted for any crimes he may have committed in office. When he'd argued that, he'd been thinking more along the lines of treason, rape, violating the emolument clause of the Constitution, and the like. Not murdering and eating people and their unborn babies in the White House before a bevy of cameras.

"What kind of medical treatment did he receive at Walter Reed?"

All eyes turned toward Nealy.

"Is this the result of that experimental stuff they gave him? The steroids and the… the whatever it was. The vaccine?"

Joanna Quigley, Secretary of Health and Human Services, shook her head. "I don't believe so, no. The treatments he received were perfectly safe, and the steroids he was given wouldn't ever lead to something like this. This is something else entirely."

"You're thinking terrorism?" Secretary of Defense Nicholas Furth asked.

"Aren't you?" Quigley shot back, one eyebrow raised.

"Oh my God," Bonny said.

Racine turned toward him, the man's face as white as a sheet, eyes staring wide. He followed Bonny's gaze to the monitors behind him, to the real-time broadcast of the Emergency Response Team's breaching of the Press Briefing Room. What he saw made no sense, though. There was only one man standing, and the Coleridges…

Oh God…

They made quick work of the last agent then began to move toward the door leading into the press corps offices.

"What's the status of the football?" Racine asked.

The football was the nickname given to the briefcase that carried mobile nuclear launch command codes. With it, the president could

authorize the use of nuclear weapons, and it traveled with him wherever he went.

Vice President Nealy traveled with his own military and communications entourage that was similar to that of the president. His military aides had their own version of the nuclear football, and Nealy had his own set of sealed launch codes that could be used to initiate a nuclear strike.

"President Coleridge's codes have been deactivated," Major Henderson said. "Vice President Nealy's football is now the primary launch device."

Racine let out a breath. That was some comfort, at least. He felt better knowing that if, somehow, Coleridge made it deeper into the West Wing, he couldn't just mosey down to the Situation Room and initiate a nuclear attack from there.

The First Family passed through the door and out of the briefing room. The cameras stared down at the carnage they had left in their wake, dispassionately broadcasting images of a sea of gutted and dismembered corpses, blood, and spilled organs.

"All right, let's take a vote," Racine said. "All in favor of transferring presidential power to Vice President Nealy?"

"Hell, he's already got the nukes," Furth said and, with fake cheer, raised his hand. "Why not?"

The fifteen principal officers of the executive departments of the cabinet cast their votes. Only Connolly objected, arguing, again, that Coleridge was clearly capable of physically exercising the powers of his office.

"Well, Mr. Vice President," Racine said. "I believe that now makes you acting president."

Racine turned back to his aide. "We got a Bible handy? And more Tums, too, please. Thanks."

EIGHT

Hutchinson's balls shriveled and tried to crawl back up into his pelvis as he watched the mayhem unfold. He felt sick, and a wave of hopelessness washed over him.

He wondered whether the First Family had ever been unconscious at all or if they'd been playing possum to lure the ERT into a false sense of security before springing their trap.

Coleridge and his clan were just as merciless with the waiting medical team as they had been with all their prior victims. On the surveillance monitor, Hutchinson watched helplessly as the president grabbed Secret Service Medical Officer Will Taggart by the face and lifted him off his feet, his fingers digging into Taggart's cheeks, his nails drawing pinpricks of blood.

The president had unusually small hands that were well out of proportion to his outsized frame. Hutchinson watched in disbelief as those hands twisted and enlarged, the fingers stretching, skin breaking as the bones of each digit grew distended and snapped apart the flesh encasing them. Coleridge's fingers transformed into long bony

knives that tapered into cruelly pointed, hooked ends.

Coleridge drew a finger up the length of Taggart's torso, slicing away the buttons of the man's shirt. He grabbed the front of the agent's Kevlar vest and tore it free to reveal the soft pale flesh beneath. He licked his lips, salivating. Hutchinson was glad he couldn't hear what the president was saying or the noises the medic was making as his legs kicked feebly in the air.

The camera feed carried no audio, and Hutchinson was grateful for that. Watching was bad enough.

The president dug his fingertips into Taggart's belly, taking his time, savoring it. Oh so slowly, those skeletal blades pierced flesh and sank deeper, to the first knuckle, then the second. His wrist rotated slightly as his hand sank in, deeper and deeper.

Taggart's head snapped back in a silent scream, pink spittle flying from his lips.

Coleridge worked his hand in farther, his forearm twisting to an upward angle until he was elbow deep in the man's belly, pushing in and up farther still, his shoulder becoming almost flush with Taggart's chest. Taggart was shaking and jittering, as if he was in the midst of a seizure. Coleridge's wriggling fingers jutted out from the inside of Taggart's mouth then curled around the fat pink worm of muscle. He seized the medic's tongue and pulled savagely. Blood sheeted out of Taggart's mouth, pouring down in a thick waterfall across his chin.

The president ripped his arm out of the massive cavity he'd made in the medic's chest, a trail of viscera and gore spilling out of the cavernous hole. Coleridge released the disemboweled man, dropping him into a pile of his own steaming organs, then flung the limp, useless tongue at him.

Hutchinson recognized the self-satisfied smirk on the president's

face and hated him all the more for it.

As Coleridge rejoined his family and stepped over the bodies of the other slaughtered medics, he was met with gunfire. Howett's backup team, too late, swarmed into the room. Despite the First Family being repeatedly struck with rubber bullets, none of them fell or even seemed perturbed by the assault to their bodies.

Hutchinson couldn't stand around and watch yet another massacre. He tore off his coat as he charged toward the armory, shoving past the requisitions officer, and began arming himself for war.

This has to end, here and now.

***

A dozen agents from the USSS Counterassault Team, clad in black protective gear and gasmasks, fired rubber bullets through a thick, hazy cloud of tear gas. The Rose Garden and the West Colonnade looked like a scene Hutchinson had seen too frequently in news broadcasts reporting on the protests that had been raging in cities across the US for months. Only, instead of shooting at protestors, the agents were firing at the president, his wife, and his children.

Smoke swirled in thick sheets across the snowy grounds. The First Family waded through the fog. Although they were bloodied and disheveled, the tear gas proved to be every bit as useless as the nonlethal ammunition. The Coleridges snarled at the line of agents, baring their gory fangs, and leapt into the fray. Only Melanie, the president's wife, stayed behind, in the shadows that covered the colonnade. Her lips were moving, and she was gesticulating oddly with her hands, but Hutchinson couldn't make out what she was saying.

Approaching from the south side of the Rose Garden, Hutchinson came at the scene perpendicularly. The sight of the newly made

war zone twisted his stomach savagely. Even more sickening were the words that left his mouth when he activated his radio to issue a command he'd never thought he would ever have to give.

"Switch to live ammo," he said. He rushed forward, opening fire on the First Family as they tore through the line of agents attempting to contain them. Radioing to the counter-sniper teams stationed atop the White House, Hutchinson ordered, "If you see a shot, take it."

He aimed through the fog, lining his gunsights up squarely with the broad chest of the president. His finger curled around the trigger, ready to squeeze and—

A massive rumble shook the ground beneath his feet, upsetting his aim. The tremor was short-lived, and Hutchinson dropped to one knee before he was knocked off his feet entirely. He watched as members of the counterassault team and the Coleridges themselves flailed and fell. Hutchinson had lost his target, and now the sprawl of bodies made it too risky to fire. Keeping close to the ground, the Coleridges moved on all fours as they sought out their victims.

"We've got movement in the Press Briefing Room," Lorn said. As he broadcast across the shared channel to all agents, Hutchinson detected a tremor of fear in his voice—small, but there nonetheless.

"What kind of movement?"

"I…" he began, but words failed him as he stammered into the radio then fell silent. A moment later, he broke the quiet and said, "They're coming your way."

With two out of the three doors into the Press Briefing Room sealed, he knew the new threats would have to follow a similar path out of the West Wing as the Coleridges'. He turned on one knee and, from behind the shallow cover of a knee-high hedgerow, took aim at the ruined doors to the Palm Room.

A moment later, Hutchinson was forced to reevaluate the scene before him. He had been wrong. This didn't look anything like the more-recent press coverages of the protests and riots against police violence. It wasn't a scene out of the news at all. It was something from a horror movie.

Those reporters who were able-bodied enough and who still possessed the legs to do so moved quickly. Armless, their faces ruined and eaten away, the members of the White House press corps pushed their way into the Rose Garden.

Among their numbers were the four-man ERT team that had been sent into the White House only moments before, along with the medical response team. Taggert shambled out from under the colonnade, the cold wind whipping at the ruins of his uniform blouse to expose the gaping, hollow cavity of his chest. As Taggert shambled onto the lawn, Hutchinson could see straight through the man's gutted abdomen to the blood-slicked spinal column at the back of the giant hole.

He fired his 9mm Glock 19, putting a fresh hole in Taggert's forehead. The dead man dropped, no longer moving. He lined up his next shot, putting a round through the eye goggle of Howett's gas mask. Howett's head snapped back, but he continued rushing forward, through the cloud of tear gas and into the fray, where he joined in on the assault against the CAT.

One journalist's head exploded, and a second later, the boom of the shot that had caused that killing blow rang out in the cold, darkening sky. From their higher vantage points along the roof of the White House, the counter-snipers were opening fire with their MK11 semi-automatic rifles as more targets filed into view and reached the open expanse of the Rose Garden lawn, no longer protected by the roof of the colonnade.

Hutchinson turned his attention toward Melanie, realizing the First Lady had not yet joined the battle. She was still under the cover of the colonnade roof and shielded by the regularly spaced federal-style pillars. Keeping low, he moved along the hedgerow until he was kitty-corner to her, close enough to the colonnade to dart behind a pillar.

He looked around the thick column and carefully took aim. He could just make out the edges of her frame. He didn't think he would be able to hit her, but he could at least flush her out.

The bullet from his Glock 19 took a chunk out of the pillar and lit a fire under the First Lady's ass. Melanie ran screaming away from her safe space and into the swirling snow. Hutchinson opened fire on her retreating form. A line of bullets tattooed their way up her rear then to a spot between her shoulder blades, sending her sprawling facedown in the snow.

The Rose Garden was littered with the bodies of twice-dead journalists and murdered Secret Service agents. Coleridge and his children had been able to push their advantage, bulling their way to the entrance of the Oval Office. They'd killed a number of the CAT and were now using the corpses as shields to protect themselves from the snipers above as they rushed across the lawn.

Coleridge charged to the patio like a rhino then hoisted the body of the CAT agent he was holding over his head. He violently threw the dead man into the white door of the Oval Office, to little effect. While much of the door consisted of framed, inset bulletproof ballistic glass, the steel door itself was less sturdy. Although much of the White House had been retrofitted with upgraded security and accompanying technology, the historical building had a certain look and feel that was expected to be preserved. Rather than tear out the door and its wooden frame then reinstall an upgraded, high-security

door that would require additional support elements for added protection, no one had replaced the door itself in a number of years. It had been considered sufficient enough for security purposes—particularly given all of the other security features and armed responses that went hand in hand with the White House—that only a second layer of ballistic glass had been installed behind the original glass. Hutchinson had advocated for the entire system to be replaced and resecured, but the administration had overruled his recommendation, stating that it would be too expensive and unnecessary. The Oval Office was protected largely by bulletproof glass, and there was a trapdoor beneath the president's desk in case an emergency evacuation was needed. It was deemed, in terms of official government policy under the Coleridge administration, "good enough."

"Who gives a shit about a fucking door?" Coleridge had pointedly argued, and because he was President of the United States, nobody had seen fit to argue the point further.

Now, Coleridge was holding a CAT officer with one hand on the back of the agent's neck and the other gripping his uniform belt, using the corpse like a battering ram. Coleridge's children, hiding behind human shields of their own, formed a ring behind him and were absorbing gunfire from the remaining counterassault team and the White House snipers.

As Hutchinson opened fire, he could hear the heavy thumps of the CAT member's helmet striking the door and the breaking of bone as the agent's neck and skull shattered under the assault. More loud thumps rose into the air, immediately followed by the sharp cracking noises of bones splintering violently. A louder commotion split the air, and he knew Coleridge was through. He couldn't find a target behind the corpse shields, which were now moving backward and into the Oval Office.

Hutchinson chased after them. As he drew near the threshold of the Oval Office, he pushed his back to the wall and glanced around the shattered door. The room was empty. On the cold patio stone, the dead CAT agent Coleridge had used to prize open the door lay dead. The body was crumpled, and broken bones stuck up through the man's clothing at odd angles all across his torso. In death, he had taken on an almost porcupine-like appearance because of the shattered pieces of ribs that stood on end, having been punched through his back.

Hutchinson took a deep breath, preparing himself to enter the Oval Office. The ground began to rumble again, a loud, angry growl filling the sky. And then all hell broke loose.

Tyler D. Coleridge

The time is NOW! RETAKE the WHITE HOUSE for AMERICA! #AmericanExceptionalism!

5:00 p.m. - 1 JAN 2021

Melanie Coleridge

The time is NOW! RETAKE the WHITE HOUSE for AMERICA! #AmericanExceptionalism!

5:00 p.m. - 1 JAN 2021

David Coleridge

The time is NOW! RETAKE the WHITE HOUSE for AMERICA! #AmericanExceptionalism!

5:00 p.m. - 1 JAN 2021

Stephen Coleridge

The time is NOW! RETAKE the WHITE HOUSE for AMERICA! #AmericanExceptionalism!

5:00 p.m. - 1 JAN 2021

Evelyn Coleridge

The time is NOW! RETAKE the WHITE HOUSE for AMERICA! #AmericanExceptionalism!

5:00 p.m. - 1 JAN 2021

<u>NINE</u>

In June, BLM protestors had marched by the hundreds on Pennsylvania Avenue, chanting for the president's removal from the White House. In response, the Secret Service had closed the streets around the People's House to pedestrian and vehicular traffic. Tall black fencing had been swiftly erected around the White House, and it stretched for several blocks along Fifteenth Street and Seventeenth Street, cordoning off Lafayette Square, to the north of the White House, on H Street and to Constitution Avenue and The Ellipse to the south. A month later, massive non-scalable walls had been built along the South Lawn of the White House. In November, days before the election, a third layer of fencing and another layer of anti-climb walls had gone up in an attempt to make the White House into an impenetrable bunker that could barely even be seen from the streets.

Stationed behind the black fencing on H Street, Agent Mendez could not see the lettering on the front of the protest signs wallpapering the street-facing side of the fence, but he knew each of them

by heart. Black Lives Matter, Trans Lives Matter, Arrest Coleridge, Coleridge Is Killing Us, Fake President, Coleridge Is a Danger to Us All, Coleridge is Sick, Coleridge is Guilty, We Will Defeat Coleridge, Remove Greed, Remove Coleridge, Coleridge is a Liar, Take Coleridge Down. The paraphernalia of a dying democracy's final days, it was accompanied by the steady stream of protesters who came daily to chant and shout their slogans in an attempt to save their country. Eight walls and a dozen fences worth of the same, and in the center of it all was the most hated man in America.

Each of the four corners of the grid of cross streets were barricaded and staffed by armed members of the USSS Counterassault Team and K9 units. For the last six months, their duties had been little more than redirecting traffic, demanding drivers turn around and for pedestrians hoping to see the heart and soul of their nation's capital to find somewhere else to be and to get there by some other route.

Those who lived and worked in DC had gradually become used to the alterations in their daily routes, thanks to the ever-growing restrictions placed upon the once-public White House. Those who were irate, though, were kept in check by the highly visible SR-16 CQB assault rifles the members of the CAT carried.

The members of the CAT brandished those very same assault rifles as the full-throated growls from packs of Harley-Davidson Fat Boys bore down on them, the motorcyclists refusing to stop as ordered. The physical display of weaponry was less a deterrent and more of a provocation, as the motorcyclists drew down on the US Secret Service agents with assault rifles of their own.

Gunfire erupted in the night as the riders opened fire on the CAT agents. The Fat Boys broke through the wooden sawhorse barricades on either side of H Street, while the men and women of the Secret Service sought cover behind their vehicles, which were angled

a few feet behind the barricades as an additional stopper.

The bikers crashed through the sawhorses and darted through the gap between the noses of the black sedans, shooting their way toward Pennsylvania Avenue.

Agent Mendez scrambled around his vehicle in search of better cover as he radioed for backup. He had seen enough of the bikers to know they belonged to the white supremacist group known as the 88 Blades, an organization that had loudly supported Coleridge in both the 2016 and 2020 elections and often acted as de facto security inside and outside of the president's many nationwide rallies, attacking protestors and police alike. Their Fat Boys flew the flag of the 88 Blades in a confused jumble of ideologies alongside the US flag, the Nazi swastika, and the Confederate Stars and Bars.

Bullets slammed into the opposite side of the sedan as Mendez returned fire over the trunk of the vehicle. The car was reinforced and bulletproof, so he wasn't concerned about gunfire from the 88 Blades hitting the gas tank and blowing him up, but he was concerned about a stray round catching him in the face. Keeping his profile as small as possible, he aimed and fired at his targets.

He caught one rider square in the back, between the shoulder blades, and watched—with just a touch of pride—as that racist fuck toppled off his Harley and skidded a dozen feet along the surface of H Street. His enjoyment was short-lived, though, as his brain finally processed what each of the riders was wearing.

To a man, the members of the 88 Blades were clad in Kevlar and wearing tactical vests and police-style helmets with clear visors over their faces. Some wore gas masks, but the attire was otherwise the same. They had come prepared and with a clear intent.

Looking to the south, Mendez saw additional riders engaging the counterassault teams stationed at the corner of Fifteenth and

Constitution, both sides pinning each other down with gunfire.

While the USSS CAT performed admirably and left members of the 88 Blades lying wounded and bleeding in the street, the simple fact was, they were outnumbered until backup could arrive.

Slowly, it dawned on Mendez that his call for backup had not been met with a response.

What the hell is—

Before he could dwell on that realization, a new sound joined the ruckus, loud and grumbling, and he looked toward the whine of a massive engine. An enormous Mack truck smashed through the barricades in the center of H Street, at the Sixteenth Street intersection, and then violently plowed its way through the heavy black sedans parked there. CAT opened fire on the Mack truck, their bullets tearing through the vehicle's grill and engine block, but the vehicle had momentum on its side. Even as one tire blew out, the Mack truck jumped a curb and slammed through the fencing closing off Lafayette Square park. It was headed directly toward the White House.

The truck was hauling a big, metal twenty-eight-and-a-half-foot trailer, and as its eighteen wheels chewed through snow and frozen mud and grass, the back of that trailer opened. Mounted inside was a Gatling-style minigun, along with dozens and dozens more of the 88 Blades.

The minigun ate through H Street and the USSS sedans. Mendez watched, helplessly, as the men and women he'd worked alongside for years were blown apart as they attempted to return fire and take out the machine gunner. Mendez himself did not have a clear line of fire, being off to the side as he was, and the semi was only getting farther away… and then the Mack truck struck the anti-climb wall head-on.

Years ago, Mendez had seen a YouTube video of a semitruck hit-

ting a concrete barrier. Now, he watched something very similar play out right before his eyes. The big red cab slammed into the unscalable wall and crumpled, reminding Mendez of a kid squeezing Play-Doh through his fingers. The entire engine block accordioned into a pancake, and glass exploded. The trailer it was hauling was jolted so badly by the sudden stopping power of the impact that it kept moving forward as it was flipped upward. Sparks ignited gasoline and oil spilling from the ruptured engine block, and a fireball exploded just as the trailer, which had hung suspended in the air for the briefest of moments, slammed back down. However many fascism-loving sardines were jammed in that tin can were rattled, but some of them still had enough sense to flee. Mendez watched as members of the 88 Blades tumbled out, stumbling and falling, clearly disoriented and completely disheveled, as they tried to get to safety.

Through it all, a dozen or so Fat Boy riders were still tearing ass along H Street, looking for stragglers, like Mendez. They circled the parked sedans, opening fire on the pinned-down agents. Tortured screams rose along with the gunfire, and Mendez swore he wouldn't go down like a bitch. He quickly shuffled behind the hood and opened fire on the nearest rider, aiming for the man's face. Although the racist fuck had a visor protecting his face, Mendez had little doubt that his ammunition would cut through it like butter. He was right, too, and he grinned as the fat boy riding the Fat Boy was blown right off his seat. The motorcycle threw up sparks as its metal body glided along the pavement then thumped heavily into the rear wheel opposite Mendez.

Then, like his fellow soldiers, he was surrounded, caught in the eye of a hurricane of angry, bitter white men armed for war. They circled him and fired. Circled and fired.

Mendez felt his ribs break beneath his Kevlar vest. Flares of pain

exploded in his arms and legs. A fresh jolt of searing pain forced him to look at the ragged stump of one leg. His brain refused to process what his eyes told him—that his leg was gone, dismembered by automatic weapons fire a third of the way down his thigh.

More bullets crashed into him as the Fat Boy riders hooted and hollered, shouting things like "Die, spic!" and "Immigrant trash!"

Mendez slumped over. A bullet slammed into the top of his trapezius and shattered his collar bone as it drove deeper into his body, unstoppable, on a path for his heart.

**

Agent Victoria Iglesias couldn't believe her eyes. Staring through the scope of her MK11 sniper rifle from the roof of the West Wing, overlooking the Rose Garden, she watched as Melanie Coleridge stood. She'd watched Melanie fall after being shot in the back by Agent Hutchinson, who'd scored at least three direct hits on FLOTUS. The snow around where Melanie had lain was stained almost black with her blood. As plain as day and crystal clear, Iglesias saw the large exit wounds that had been torn open across the First Lady's chest and the front of her clothes.

Then she saw Melanie's bright-yellow eyes and the large liquidy black pupil in the center. The First Lady's eyes roiled strangely, the cloudy fluid of her sclera shifting and churning around the unusually large black center, the eye of this oddly colored storm. The skin of her face was cracked and leathery, almost reptilian in appearance. Her pale countenance had taken on a dusky hue, and patchy clumps of her once-thick and expensively styled blond hair had fallen away. Strange, bumpy ridges and unnatural pointed protrusions of bone were visible along the top of her skull where her hair had sloughed

off.

Melanie stalked toward the counterassault team fighting on the lawn. Iglesias's finger began to squeeze the trigger, but a flash of movement made her pause.

Melanie's hands... had mutated into sharp, bony talons, her fingers much longer than they had once been. The journalists—the *dead* journalists, Iglesias's mind corrected—were similarly disfigured.

What was perhaps worse, if this nightmare scenario could somehow manage to get even worse, was that members of the counterassault team, men and women she knew had been killed only moments ago, were beginning to rise.

But that's impossible.

Agent Golden's throat had been bitten out, and beneath his chin was a gaping tear deep enough that Iglesias could make out the ridges of vertebrae in the back of the man's neck. *No way should he be standing.*

The same applied to President Coleridge and his clan. Iglesias had seen the counterassault team open fire on the entire First Family, mowing them down. It had been absolutely insane, one of the most batshit, out-there, "what the fuck is happening?" moments of not just Iglesias's career but of her entire fucking life. The Secret Service had turned on the president and his family and killed them! And then Coleridge and his children had started moving despite their wounds, moving with inhuman agility as they began killing the counterassault team with their bare hands! And now the president's wife, who had most certainly been dead, was moving as if she'd never been shot at all. And not just moving but moving *inhumanly fast.*

This shouldn't be happening. None of it.

And yet...

Iglesias shook her head, trying to recenter her focus on the here

and now. Of the Coleridges, only Melanie was still in the Rose Garden. Most of the dead journos were back to being dead again, and Iglesias and her fellow snipers had taken out the resurrected members of the CAT team.

The Rose Garden had been turned into a goddamned cemetery, with corpses littering it from one end to the other. The counterassault team had been decimated, and the handful of agents who were still fighting were engaged in combat against a score of... *What, exactly? Zombies?*

Iglesias lined up her rifle to Melanie Coleridge's head, the center of the crosshairs affixed to the dead center of her deformed skull. The wind caught the ends of the First Lady's limp hair and pulled the remaining handfuls free, exposing all the knobs and ridges of her oddly shaped and bony cranium.

Iglesias's mind seized on the word for what the Coleridges were. What they had become. What they, the journos, and the CAT team members had all transformed into. They were demons.

On any other day, Iglesias would have scoffed at such an idea. What she'd seen this evening, though... It was impossible to laugh. It was also the only thing that made any sense at all. She could hear her abuela's voice in her head even now, telling her these people were demonios, that they were nahuals, or at least close enough, all of them de fuerza negra. And believing that much of the crowd below her were inhuman, that they were, in fact, monsters, made pulling the trigger all the easier.

Still, she prayed for strength, as silently and quickly as she could, as her finger tightened around the trigger. Her body absorbed the recoil, and she stared through the scope to confirm her kill.

Melanie Coleridge, impossibly, was gone. Lightning fast, she had moved a hair's breadth away at the moment prior to the trig-

ger pull, and she was darting toward the wall. Because Iglesias had claimed Melanie as her own target, the other snipers were focusing on supporting the assault team on the ground and radioing in updates as their targets fell—and then got back up and attacked anybody in reach who wasn't already a demon, only to fall again a brief time later.

Iglesias tracked Melanie's ascent up the wall. The thick, pointed claws at the end of her malformed hands punched into the brick, and she scrabbled upward with spider-like rapidity. Iglesias had missed once already, and she didn't intend to do so a second time. She let the rifle lead Melanie a bit, firing at the place where the First Lady should have been, at the exact moment she should have been there. But Melanie moved again, swiftly darting to safety just as Iglesias pulled the trigger to end her.

Melanie pushed up off the wall, leaping onto the roof and into the center of the sniper's nest opposite Iglesias. In the time it took her to realign her rifle sights, Melanie had already torn apart the CS agent stationed there. The wicked fingers of one hand stabbed through Leslie Hyde's eyes, while the others punched through Kevlar and spine. Melanie hoisted the body overhead and pitched Hyde off the roof.

Taking a knee, Iglesias fired again, hitting Melanie center mass.

Melanie backpedaled then looked at the sniper, smiling across the gap. Her teeth were shark-like, sharp and jagged, clustered in rows that defied human biology. The woman's jawline had elongated to accommodate the proliferation of bloody teeth.

Iglesias fired and, again, missed. Her cheeks puffed as she let out an angry, frustrated breath. She sought out her target again, only to find FLOTUS rushing directly at her. Melanie threw herself into Iglesias, her arms wrapping around the agent's waist, and sent both

of them flying off the roof.

All of the air in Iglesias's lungs left in a rush, and pain torqued her body. A muscle spasm ripped through her back, and when they'd hit the earth, Melanie's knee had bounced hard into her belly. She felt sick and faint, her head swimming from rattling around inside her helmet following her collision with the snow-packed frozen ground. It took her a moment to regain focus, already certain she'd been concussed in the fall. But it was too late by then.

The First Lady slithered atop Iglesias's body, straddling her hips. Her hands reached for the agent's throat, those elongated, bony, strangely jointed digits curling around Iglesias's slender brown neck as if they were lovers. When she smiled and revealed those nightmarish teeth, her leathery, tautly stretched skin cracked apart and oozed a viscous, stinking, pus-colored liquid. She lapped at the foul secretion with a long, slender forked tongue. Her grip tightened around Iglesias's neck, her nails drawing pinpricks of blood, and her hips began grinding against her prey.

Melanie moaned as a pungent, roadkill-like stench rose from her body. The hooked point of her thumb dug into the hollow of Iglesias's throat. Two things occurred to Victoria Iglesias in that moment. The first was that smell of rodent decay wafting from the First Lady was the heady musk of arousal, and it was growing stronger the more turned on she became. As she approached her climax, the air grew thick with the stink of hundreds of dead mice, and what little air Iglesias was able to drag in as Melanie Coleridge's massive hands clamped off her esophagus made her gag, an acidic streak of bile rising in her throat.

The second realization was that she could reach her backup piece, a SIG Sauer P229 that was strapped to her thigh, right beside the curve of Melanie's calf. As she moved for the gun, FLOTUS

smiled, perhaps thinking Iglesias was trying to cop a deathbed feel.

The First Lady's lusty putrescence grew headier, and a thick wetness splashed against the crotch of Iglesias's combat pants as FLOTUS came, her hands becoming a vise around the sniper's neck, pinching off her air supply entirely.

Blood rushed to Iglesias's cheeks, turning her entire face hot, and the corners of her vision turned pitch-black. The noise of her pulse was thunderous in her ears, and her tongue felt suddenly thick and heavy as it bulged from between her lips.

Her arm was impossibly heavy, and the movement sent lightning bolts of pain all along her back. She fought through the incredible ache and slammed the muzzle of the P229 against Melanie Coleridge's temple. This close, there was no way for her to dodge the bullet.

Iglesias pulled the trigger and watched through darkening vision as the skin around Melanie's right eye briefly ballooned outward under the concussive force of the gun's explosive gases. It rippled back into place like a calming sea, and the left side of her skull exploded outward in a shower of blood, brains, and bone.

Half a second later, the First Lady's body fell limply to the side. Iglesias gasped for air, her lungs burning and throat aching. The front of her pants were covered in a greasy, foul discharge, as if somebody had just smeared a rotting, bloated squirrel across her lap.

She looked at the corpse of Melanie Coleridge and, entirely certain the woman was finally, really, actually dead this time, spit on her. "You are one ugly, nasty-ass bitch, you know that?"

Slowly, painfully, she worked her way onto her side. Something inside her, running up and down the length of her spine, was all fucked up, and every inch of movement was complete agony. Sweat burst across her forehead; the pain was so great that she thought she

was going to throw up, but she kept working her body. She got one knee under herself then used that and the nearest pillar of the Colonnade as support to push up and onto her feet.

Lights flashed across the ground, coming in over President's Park and sweeping over the South Lawn on approach to the White House. Still dazed from the fall and in a hell of a lot of pain, it took her a moment to place what that distinct and highly recognizable sound was. A helicopter.

As Iglesias lurched out of the reach of the aerial floodlights, she radioed for backup. There was no response.

***

Lee Ridgewood, chairman of the 88 Blades, grinned from the passenger seat of the McDonnell Douglas MD 500 helicopter as it dove toward the South Lawn of the White House. Below, all he could see was smoke and the brilliant bursts of gunfire, and it made him smile. His smile grew bigger as the chopper's enormous floodlights illuminated the contours of the Oval Office.

The Oval Office was exactly where Ridgewood was headed. He planned to secure and hold it, with the help of his truckful of men, until President Coleridge was found and was safe enough to reclaim it.

He spoke over the helicopter radio to the three men—the Elder Chapter of the 88 Blades—packed tightly in the back with their gear. He got a copy as a response and listened to the muffled thumping of the rotor blades whirling. The floodlight was the first thing to explode, but it had served its purpose well enough. A moment later, a louder noise pushed through the air as the door-side men opened fire with their skid-mounted miniguns.

The bulletproof glass in front of Ridgewood made a loud *pock!* as a sniper's round embedded itself in the glass. More shots came, and one of their landing lights shattered. The pilot, Mitch Zoeller, swooped over the roof of the White House to give the gunners a better chance of clearing out the Secret Service counter snipers.

Unfortunately, one of those snipers got awfully lucky. A loud metallic wang and a shower of sparks rattled the cabin, and some kind of hydraulic hose smacked the glass next to Ridgewood's head.

"I can't keep her up!" Zoeller shouted into the radio.

Ridgewood could see him struggling with the cyclic, trying to control the helicopter's descent, but it was clearly useless.

"All right, brace yourself," he shouted.

More sparks lit up the cabin as sniper rounds shot through the underbelly of the MD 500, and a control panel filled with all kinds of gauges blew. The windscreen was littered with large concentric circles, and at the center of each were the copper bullet shells stopped by the bullet-resistant glass. More rings were forming as the window absorbed additional sniper fire from the White House roof.

The helicopter spun out of control, and the whole damn world went all tilt-a-whirl. All Ridgewood could see were contrails of rapidly spinning white. The blades hit something big and hard, and the whole copter shook, rattled, and bounced as it barreled through the edge of the West Colonnade's roof and played pinball between the row of thick pillars below. The tail of the MD 500 sheared off, and as the cabin began to lose momentum, Ridgewood saw it flip and stab into the frozen ground of the Rose Garden lawn. The cabin slammed through another pillar and onto the snow-covered ground. The metal underbelly cut through the snow as it ground its way to a stop, finally coming to a rest and canting unevenly, having lost both landing skids somewhere along the way.

Ridgewood smelled gas and fire, and his heart was racing. *Goddamn! Now that was a fucking rush!*

He wanted to shout and whoop as he punched the ceiling, but he kept himself in check. Instead, he spared a moment to take stock of his body, pressing his hands against his legs, chest, and crotch. Satisfied all his vitals were in place, he shoved open his door and brought his assault rifle up, notching the wooden stock into his shoulder. Visibility was shot. The air was thick with dust and smoke from the ruins of the West Colonnade, the MD 500, and thickening snowfall. The weather was turning lousier and lousier by the second.

Above him, somebody grunted and fell off the chunks of decimated Colonnade roof that was now heaped up in piles against the walls of the White House and scattered on the lawn. A black-clad man landed ungainly at Ridgewood's feet—a sniper, he realized, one of the cockroaches who'd been stationed up on the roof. The sniper's face was a bloody mess, and his leg was broken. Jagged white bone stuck up at a sharp angle through the man's pants.

Ridgewood smiled at the prospect of such an easy kill. It boded well for the rest of their night. He was shocked at just how easy breaching the White House perimeter had been, in fact. For all the lore surrounding the security of this place, he would have thought it would be more of a challenge. Granted, his enemies certainly had the manpower, but the men of the 88 Blades were better.

So much for all that government training. He couldn't help but laugh.

He raised his rifle and fired a round into the sniper's throat. Then he listened for a moment, enjoying the wet burbling noise the man made as he choked to death on own his blood. It was kind of funny, he thought.

Ridgewood watched as the Elder Chapter of the 88 Blades

fanned out across the Rose Garden, shooting at everyone still moving. *Some of these people, though… Christ!* Looking at them, he wasn't sure how they even managed. There was one dude in a brown suit, missing both arms and his lower jaw, trying to dig his teeth into an armored government thug. Clete Wittig punched that bastard's clock with a three-round burst to the head then did the same to the government boy. *Now, how's that for their tax dollars at work?*

Whistling softly to himself, Ridgewood turned toward the Rose Garden, wanting to break off a piece or two for himself. He stood stock-still, unable to believe his eyes as some Asian bitch stalked toward him. How this slanty-eyed whore was moving at all left him dumbfounded. A giant cavity had been torn into her tummy, leaving behind only a hollow, gutless hole. Her color was all wrong, too, for an Oriental. She was browner than she should've been, as if her shadow had crawled up under her skin. Her face looked strange, also, like the bottom half had been pulled straight down and out to either side so that her jowls were wider than the top of her head. Her eyes burned an angry yellow, and Ridgewood swore he could see the flicker of flame dancing into those oddly colored orbs.

He fired, the rifle hip-high, and watched as more holes opened up in her torso. She danced a jitterbug, and he fired some more, his rounds blasting her arm off just below the elbow.

Ridgewood wondered briefly if she were on PCP.

Or maybe it's all that MSG, he thought, laughing. She kept approaching, and he kept firing, tearing away chunks of meat from her legs and shoulders. Bullets slammed into her chest, finally toppling her off balance.

You ain't no Jackie Chan, that's for damn sure!

He looked around for his pals, wanting to share that joke with them and hear their laughter. But as he sought out his compatriots,

he realized things had gone terribly, terribly wrong while he'd been playing with the Chinawoman.

He met Zoeller's eyes, then Niebling's, Wittig's, and Kaste's. Their eyes were… all wrong. They'd all been bitten, too, in the throat or on the face. Billy Kaste—Ol' BK, the Whopper himself—was missing three fingers, the skin shredded where they'd been bitten off.

Fingers curled around Ridgewood's ankle, and something tugged violently at the bottom of his blue jeans, around his calf. He looked, even as he winced from the tight pinching pain there, and saw a black-clad man with a fucked-up leg. Behind this guy was a long red streak that led all the way back to the helicopter.

Ridgewood's jean leg tore, and the cold wind shocked his warm skin. He tried to shake loose from the man's grip then kicked himself free, colliding with something cold and hard. A startled cry tore loose from him as he came face-to-face with that Asian bitch again. As fast as an angry snake, her hand darted out and grabbed him by the throat.

Her teeth—incredibly wrong-looking teeth, he noted—snapped at his face, tearing loose a chunk of skin beneath one eye. Her hooked nails punched into either side of his throat. Warm blood sprayed against her face. More gushed out, spreading heat down his chest and soaking his shirt. Another set of teeth bit into the muscle of his calf, the head of the impatient eater shaking violently to pull the meat off the bone.

The Elder Chapter pressed their bodies to his, and more razor-sharp teeth dug into his back and belly on either side of his hips. Through his darkening vision, he watched helplessly as Billy Kaste's jaw unhinged and a ropy, foot-long tongue tasted the air. Kaste sank to his knees and out of sight. Ridgewood didn't need to see what the man was intending, though. He felt it plainly enough. Kaste's point-

ed teeth bit through the crotch of Ridgewood's pants, into the delicate, tender flesh that joined his cock and testicles to his body, and ripped them away. Blood sheeted down the insides of Ridgewood's thighs, and he could hear the click of Kaste's throat as he swallowed. Then Kaste's head was back, burrowing into the freshly made hole, his teeth carving a deeper tunnel into Ridgewood's core.

Ridgewood spent his final moments screaming to death. Even over the sounds of his own pain, he could hear the snicking and clacking of teeth and the noisy sounds of meat being lustily chewed. When the woman finally released him from her clutches, his dying body sank into the deep-red snow blanketing the Rose Garden.

Moments later, Ridgewood's body rose. It was not Lee Ridgewood, chairman of the 88 Blades, who was in control, though.

TEN

HUTCHINSON PUSHED QUICKLY THROUGH THE broken door and into the Oval Office, moving for cover behind the Resolute desk. The large oak desk was probably the most well-known artifact of the Oval Office, given to President Rutherford B. Hayes by the Queen of England in 1880 and built from the timbers of the British Arctic exploration ship *HMS Resolute*. It was thick and sturdy, older even than the Oval Office, which hadn't been added onto the White House until 1909, under the orders of President William H. Taft.

Like the other Secret Service agents, Hutchinson rarely ever entered the Oval Office, let alone found himself behind the Resolute desk. On a normal day, he and another agent would be stationed outside the office, usually with the doors closed. Weight-sensitive pressure pads under the rose-colored carpet of the Oval Office let them know where the president was within the confines of the office at all times, though.

Hutchinson didn't need the pressure pads to tell him that, aside from the murdered CAT agents who had been tossed to the floor like

trash, the room was empty. From behind the thick, rounded corner of the Resolute desk, he took a quick survey of the Oval Office. The door leading to the main hallway of the West Wing was open, and fresh sets of wet footprints stained the carpeting in that direction.

Keeping low, he took cover beside the door and peeked out. Then he felt a change in the room behind him, a shift of air perhaps, the sense of a presence he'd somehow missed. Whatever it was, it made that ancient lizard part of his brain tingle and raised the hairs on the back of his neck. He took another look around the room, detecting an odd smell he hadn't noted moments ago. Something wet and heavy landed in his hair, and he looked up, toward the presidential seal on the ceiling.

His mouth fell open at the sight of Stephen Coleridge scrabbling across the smooth white surface above, hooked fingers digging into the plaster. Stephen's face was as oddly deformed as his hands, his skin looking much like a broken mug that had been sloppily pieced back together. Between the gaps of his broken flesh—Hutchinson wanted to call them scales, but that word didn't seem to fit quite right for what he was seeing—a thick, off-white liquid dripped free.

Hutchinson moved before he got splattered again. He had no idea what that off-putting liquid coming out Stephen's face was, but he was damn sure he didn't want any more of it getting on him.

As Hutchinson shoved away from the door, Stephen kicked away from the ceiling and slammed down atop him. Hutchinson hit the floor hard but recovered fast enough to send an elbow into the side of Stephen's face as he rolled beneath the president's son and shook himself free.

Stephen, unfortunately, was faster, grabbing Hutchinson by the front of his tactical vest and hauling him off the floor. Effortlessly, he then threw Hutchinson across the room.

A sharp crack of pain lit up Hutchinson's back as he collided with the top edge of the Resolute, then he slid across the surface to thump back down onto the carpet. The president's large leather chair shot backward on its casters as he fell between it and the desk, his legs tangled in the cords of the telephone sets that had been stationed atop the Resolute.

Before he could get his feet back under him, Stephen was on top of him again. Hutchinson only just barely got an arm up in time to block the sweep of the other man's wicked claws. A jagged nail dragged over one cheek, drawing a line of fire across his face.

As they scuffled on the floor, Stephen kicked the chair out of the way, and Hutchinson scrabbled away, pushing with his heels. But, again, he was too slow. Stephen grabbed him by the back of his belt and pinned him against the carpet beside the dark cherrywood table squatting beneath the Oval Office's bulletproof windows.

Somewhere along the way, Hutchinson had lost his firearm. He wished for it desperately as Stephen snarled at him. The putrid, coppery stink of his awful breath washed over Hutchinson. Stephen's claw-like hand turned into a fist, which rammed into Hutchinson's face like a battering ram. Immediately, he saw stars as his nose shattered and blood filled his mouth.

Hutchinson groped for anything that might help, his fingers dancing over unfamiliar, cold metal lines. He wasn't sure what it was, but he grabbed it and, as hard as he could, slammed it into the side of Stephen's face.

The president's son howled in pain, releasing Hutchinson as his hand flew up to his bleeding head. Blood poured out from between the fingers he'd placed over his temple. Hutchinson hit him again, harder, and heard the satisfying crack of bone. Stephen sank to one knee, his yellow eyes turning upward in his skull to show the white-

and-black-streaked undersides.

Finally, Hutchinson got a good look at his improvised weapon—a bronze bust of Thomas Jefferson. Coleridge had once told the press he'd kept this sculpture on the table behind his desk so he could always feel the eyes of one of America's most famous Founding Fathers watching him and so that he was always reminded of the work he was doing on behalf of America. Like everything else that came out of Coleridge's mouth, it was all bullshit.

Hutchinson brought the bronze statue down atop the crown of Stephen's head. A tendril of blood came away from the man's head as he raised it again then slammed it back down—again and again and again. Rotted skin split open and spilled putrescent white gore and dark-red blood, and bone shattered.

Stephen Coleridge was dead, his brain spilling out of his destroyed cranium in a chunky soup across the soft pink carpeting. Hutchinson forced his fingers to relax, and the heavy statue hit the ground with a soft thump. The head of Thomas Jefferson rolled to one side as if to turn his gaze away from such awfulness.

When he'd been thrown across the room, Hutchinson had lost his grip on the Glock, and the weapon had gone flying. He found it under one of the couches in the social meeting area ahead of the Resolute and, now confident the room had indeed been cleared of threats, cautiously looked into the corridor outside the Oval Office.

He'd seen enough awful things this evening that the long streamers of blood staining the walls in Jackson Pollock fashion and the entrails decorating the hallway carpeting from the torn apart agents hardly fazed him. Flies had lit upon the bodies, and shifting black clouds circled the corpses, their buzzing loud and nerve-rattling. Hutchinson knew each of the four dead people, one of whom was slumped against the sealed door to the chief of staff's office. The oth-

ers, or what remained of them at least, were messily scattered to the western and northern reaches of the narrow hall. They looked like broken toys strewn across the floor during an angry toddler's tantrum.

Then the eyes of one dead agent opened, the whites surrounding his pupil a putrid yellow. Hutchinson recognized the man—Kevin Whitta—and he'd been torn in half at the waist. Trailing a shattered length of spine and cords of intestine behind him, Whitta slowly dragged himself along the floor toward Hutchinson. As his nails bit into the carpet, his teeth chomped at the empty air between them.

Hutchinson raised his Glock and fired a round directly into the crown of Whitta's head. The skull slumped on a dead neck, his cheek smacking against the floor, lifeless.

Hutchinson shook his head, as if to clear away the imagery of what he'd seen and the guilt of what he'd done. His eyes surveyed the other fallen agents. The rest of the dead remained dead, and he realized they all shared significant head trauma to one degree or another. The bodies were decapitated, or their skulls had been pulverized.

He'd seen enough shitty zombie movies and episodes of *The Walking Dead* to put it together. He knew what he would have to do from here on out, even if he hated the idea with every ounce of his being.

Behind him, bright lights lit up the windows of the Oval Office and threw the chaos of the corridor into stark contrast. Moments later, the entire West Wing shook under an assault of shrieking metal, exploding brick, and the heady stink of gasoline.

Hutchinson had no idea what the fuck had just happened, but whatever it was, he had to trust that the snipers positioned topside and the counterassault teams would have it covered. His priority was finding Coleridge and putting an end to this nightmare. Bloody

footprints led him north, past the Cabinet Room and the press secretary's office, and down the stairway to the ground floor.

***

Gregg Lorn was the proud father of three—two sons and one daughter. Each of his kids had been born roughly two years apart, and
Lisa, the oldest, was nine going on thirty. Sometimes, her know-it-all
attitude could be exasperating, but most of the time, it was absolutely endearing, as if he were getting a much-too-soon glimpse of the
woman she would become. He loved all of his kids, of course, but
Lisa had a special place in his heart. She'd been his first child, and
she was Daddy's little girl all the way. She knew it, too, and had him
wrapped completely around her little finger, but he was wise to that.
He would do anything for any one of his children, sacrifice whatever
he had to in order to keep them safe. And if anything ever happened
to them, he would raze the earth in revenge and burn down the
whole world to deliver justice in their names.

Gregg Lorn was a selfless and loving father. Perhaps that was
why he couldn't believe what the president of the United States was
telling him.

Tyler Coleridge stood on the other side of the thick, bulletproof
glass door of the White House Secret Service Command Center, one
strange and wicked looking hand hooked around the throat of his
youngest son, eleven-year-old Maddock.

"Open the door and let us in, or I kill the boy," Coleridge said.
His face was tilted up toward a hidden surveillance camera that, by
all rights, he shouldn't even have known was there.

None of the Coleridges looked right, not by any estimation. To
a one, they each looked like they were suffering from a host of skin

disorders, on top of eye infections and premature hair loss.

Lorn's youngest son, George, had come down with impetigo when he was an infant. The boy had had rashes all over his face, and nasty looking blisters on his scalp and the back of his neck. The blisters had popped easily, and a honey-colored discharge had seeped out. Poor George's head had damn near been covered in crust from the infection.

Each one of the Coleridges looked like they had even more severe cases of impetigo, on top of psoriasis and maybe a few cases of skin cancer for good measure. Where they were balding, Lorn could see leaking carbuncles on their scalps, but the carbuncles looked more like stumpy fingers lodged beneath the skin, reaching for release.

His mouth went dry, and he swallowed loudly.

"I won't tell you again," Coleridge said. For emphasis, he grabbed Maddock by the back of the head and slammed the boy's face into the glass door. The eleven-year-old's nose burst, and the impact split open his forehead, leaving behind thick splatters of red-and-yellowish swirls. The boy had bitten his lip or tongue, as well, and blood trickled down his chin to join the river pouring from his nostrils.

David Coleridge laughed. The cackling was like nails on a chalkboard, and the sharp, rippling shiver it sent up the length of Lorn's spine made his shoulder twitch as he tried to duck away from the noise.

Some possessed a certain cruelty they never outgrew. Lorn thought of the way George had laughed from his high chair one lunch summers ago, when the middle child, Teddy, had been goofing around at the kitchen table. Teddy had refused to sit on his butt and was bouncing around on his knees on the seat when he got carried away and accidentally kicked the chair out from under himself. Teddy's lips smacked against the corner of the table on his way to

the floor. Lorn remembered the shock of seeing his boy bleeding for the first time, but even more than that, he remembered George's infectious laughter as if his wounded brother were the funniest thing he'd ever seen. Although Lorn knew the laughter wasn't born out of malice, he couldn't help but chide the infant with a stern rebuke.

"That isn't funny," he'd told George, more harshly than he'd intended.

Rather than give David a somber reminder of his misplaced funny bone, though, President Coleridge smiled. His teeth were small and looked like they'd each been filed to a point, and there were rows upon rows of them, as if he had a mouthful of rusty serrated knives.

That smile was what had ultimately made Lorn hit the override controls on the Command Center door, for it promised even more violence to be delivered upon the youngest member of the Coleridge family. Lorn couldn't for the life of him abide that, not in good conscience. Whatever was wrong with the boy—hell, whatever was wrong with that entire family—Lorn thought there was still a chance they could be treated, that they could be helped. The boy in particular. He was so young, for God's sake. If there was any way of helping Maddock, he had to try.

Unfortunately, it was an effort that had always been doomed from the start. As the locks disengaged and the electronic servos assisted the opening of the heavy door, Tyler Coleridge's enormous claws ripped out Maddock's throat. A geyser of blood painted the glass red, and the boy gurgled and choked on his own plasma. Coleridge tossed the child away, and the president's daughters, Diana and Christie, set upon the boy with teeth and claws, making fast work of his small body. Immobilized, the girls then began stomping on Maddock's head until his skull was little more than a slick, pasty mess on the floor.

Too late, Lorn realized his mistake, and he knew there would be no coming back from it.

He pulled his sidearm even as he was turning toward the Coleridges, and the Command Center exploded into chaos. The president's children—what was left of them, anyway, Lorn thought grimly—leapt into the fray. They bit and chewed their way through the agents stationed inside, while the president headed straight for Lorn.

"I want you to shut down all security," Coleridge said. He got right up into Lorn's personal space, his face leering, practically nose to nose.

"I will not, sir," Lorn said.

The president snorted, rolled his eyes, then looked around, arms to his sides, as if he couldn't believe what Lorn was saying.

Coleridge put an alien, cracking, peeling hand on Lorn's shoulder and gave it a gentle squeeze as he nodded. Then he quickly spun Lorn around and shoved the Secret Service agent into the bank of monitors, pinning him there.

Lorn felt sharp nails dig into his waist, searching for the buckle of his belt, which was quickly pulled loose. His pants were torn off his hips, and he could feel the president's erection growing against his backside.

Oh my God, Lorn thought, as it became clear to him how his final moments on earth would be spent. "Please, no," he sputtered. He tried to wriggle away and swung his arms behind himself in an effort to dislodge himself from the president's grip, but it was no use. Coleridge was too strong, and the weight of his body kept Lorn pressed into place.

As a panicked sweat began to bead across his forehead, cool air caressed the backs of his thighs and buttocks as his underwear was

ripped away.

"No, no, no," he said, trying to kick his way free. Rather than give him room to maneuver, his kicking only made things worse.

President Coleridge caught Lorn's flailing leg and hooked his elbow beneath the man's knee, pushing his thigh up. Lorn felt horribly exposed, and hot tears ran down his face, mingling with the warmth of the monitor the side of his face was pressed painfully against. Coleridge's erection brushed the back of Lorn's testes then—

"No!" Lorn screamed, his protest catching in his throat as he choked on the agony of muscle bruising and tender flesh tearing.

Coleridge pumped his hips hard and fast. Lorn cried as the president violently shoved farther inside. Lorn's bleeding anus lubricated the deformed monster's cock, allowing him to thrust harder and deeper.

As the president raped Lorn, he began to grunt, driving the agent's face harder into the plasma display panels until the surface cracked. Jagged points of glass cut into Lorn's cheeks, tearing through flesh to grind against his teeth.

"Shut it all down, Lorn," Coleridge said. "Shut it down now. I can make this worse, Lorn. So, so much worse. Tremendously worse, believe me."

"Go to hell," Lorn said, spitting the words out from between clenched lips. The sound of the president's flabby thighs smacking Lorn's buttocks and the weight of his balls slapping Lorn's tight sack was nearly enough to break him, to drive him insane, but he refused.

Coleridge's ruddy face leaned in close, his lips nearly touching the side of Lorn's mouth as he grunted loudly into the agent's ear. From the corner of his eye, Lorn saw something dark shift inside the president's mouth, and his eyes widened as he realized what it was. A big, fat bottle fly poked its head out from between Coleridge's gaping

lips, its body bridged across a front tooth and the pale, cracked lower lip, close enough to hear its buzzing as it took flight.

Lorn shut his eyes then and tried to think of his children, of their warmth and their love. He tried to escape into a happy place, where he could be with his kids one last time, even if it was only in his imagination. Tears leaked out from between tightly compressed eyelids. He tried to flee somewhere beyond the reach of President Coleridge, away from the embarrassing and agonizing feel of the man's small cock violating his rectum. He thought of the days spent with his kids at the park and at the zoo, their joy on Christmas morning, and the milestone of Lisa's fifth birthday.

But then a fresh pain tore Lorn away from those sweet, sweet memories. Both of Coleridge's hands pressed against either side of his skull, then his eyes imploded beneath the press of those deranged claws as they hooked around the inside of his skull and began to pull.

"Shut it down, Lorn," Coleridge said again, grunting as he fucked the man harder and faster.

Lorn was in too much pain to feel the heat of his blood leaking along the insides of his thighs. The president's hands were wrapped around Lorn's skull, his fingers *inside* his skull, and he was pulling, slowly prizing apart the agent's cranial sutures. He thrust and pulled, thrust and pulled.

Lorn felt skin tear as his scalp came apart under the rusty nails of the president's hands and bone snapping like dry kindling. He screamed blindly through the web of claws, his heart racing in panic and fear, and then—

***

Lorn's head was ripped in half, his face hanging in ragged tatters

against the broken bone. Blood washed over the monitors as his bisected brains slipped loose and smacked wetly against the floor.

Coleridge tossed aside both halves of that loser's cranium then gripped the warm corpse by the hips as he thrust wildly once more… twice…

"Ungh!" he shouted, pounding one last time and emptying his balls into the dead man's bloody, torn-up asshole.

Spent, his filthy dick slipped free as it went soft, and he pulled up his underwear and pants. His garments were stained and smelly, but he didn't care. He was the president of the United States.

He looked at the disheveled Command Center and the corpses that lay at his feet and at the feet of his children. He smiled, a rare genuine smile. Because that was what all this was about, being president. This power. So, so much power. And he was never going to give it up. Not ever.

Evelyn shoved a man in front of him—another one of the Secret Service rats that lived in these old, ugly walls. He'd been tuned up pretty good, too, and already, his lips and one eye were starting to puff and bruise.

Coleridge made the man look at Lorn. "You saw all that, did you?"

Stiffly, the man nodded.

"You can go like him, like a nasty little whore, or you can go quick. Shut down the security protocols, kill the comms grid, and I'll let you go quick. Whaddya say?"

"I… I'll do it. Sir."

Coleridge patted the man on the cheek with one gnarly, blistered claw, leaving behind a gory handprint. "Atta boy!"

Nodding toward the banks of controls that operated the White House and its entire defensive capabilities, he let the agent step for-

ward. After a few keystrokes, it was done. Unbelievable. It was pathetic how easy that was, Coleridge thought.

Coleridge gave his best, smuggest smile then turned his back on the man. "Girls, he's all yours. David, you're with me."

***

As he rounded that last corner in the stairwell and pushed into the hallway outside the Secret Service Command Center, the stench of blood and excrement hit Hutchinson square in the face and nearly set him back on his heels. As he raised his Glock, he turned his head slightly to breathe into the crook of his shoulder, hoping to filter out the rancid stink of death, but the coppery tang and fecal odors were too thick to ignore.

Dead eyes turned toward him, and he realized that wasn't quite right after all. There was life in those eyes, and they burned with an evil intensity, controlling the vacated shells of the men and women this alien life now inhabited. Hutchinson just had to cut those marionette strings by further defiling these bodies with a bullet to their heads.

Torn throats, sliced-open faces, gouged-out eyes, rent and empty bellies—he had known these dozen people in life, but death had made them strangers and transformed them strangely.

They came for him quickly, scuttling across the floor and scaling the walls to crawl across the ceiling, hoping to take him from above. He opened fire, even as he noticed the trio of familiar women farther down the hall—the president's daughters, each with a wicked, sparkling gleam in their eyes and misplaced smiles he didn't like the looks of at all.

He had dispatched three of the undead when a fourth leapt

forward from a crouch on the floor and swung dagger-like fingers across his chest. He was grateful for the vest, but those claws found unprotected skin anyway as they ripped at his jacket and dress shirt, opening up fiery lines across his biceps. He danced away, fired, then shot at another target, moving backward toward the stairwell he'd just come out of.

Hutchinson was outnumbered, and the dead were fast. Snarling mouths and bared, spit-slickened teeth pushed him farther back. A hole blossomed in the cranium of the closest agent, but Hutchinson hadn't fired. Footsteps pounded down the hall, gunfire echoing loudly through the stairwell.

"On your six!" a woman shouted from the riser above and behind him. He took a knee then shot another agent just as their head poked around the top of a doorframe.

Bodies clogged the entrance, creating a logjam as they all tried to shove through at once, their bloodlust clearly overriding any logic or planning. Hutchinson was able to breathe easier as he and the second shooter picked off their targets.

Finally, he was able to turn and see who was above him. He recognized her, but that was about it. Slowly, clearly in pain and struggling, she hobbled down the steps toward him and stopped a few risers up so they were eye level to each other.

She must have recognized his look of incomprehension and stuck her hand out to him. "Iglesias."

He shook her hand and nodded. "Hutchinson. Thank you." Her name struck a chord with him, and the missing pieces fell into place. "Victoria, right? You're supposed to be topside."

She shrugged. "Had a little fall. Besides, there's not much roof left where I was at."

Hutchinson remembered the sounds of shrieking metal and ex-

ploding plaster and glass and wondered what the hell kind of stories she had. Crusts of dried blood stained the openings of her nose and ears, and each step she took made her wince.

"Need some help?" he said, putting an arm out to help support her.

She shook her head then hobbled off the last step.

"What the fuck is going on here?" she asked.

Quickly, he filled her in with what little he knew. As they stepped over dead, brutalized bodies and waded through gore, she told him about the attack on the building's perimeter and how communications were shot. When she got to the part about Melanie Coleridge, Hutchinson said, "Shit, I thought I got her."

"Sorry."

"No, no," he said. "It's good."

Looking into the Command Center, Hutchinson said, "I guess that explains why comms aren't working."

The heart of the White House's security and command hub for the Secret Service agents stationed in and around the building was destroyed. It looked like a bomb had gone off inside, shattering the various workstations and their accompanying monitors. Only a few bodies were left inside, too ruined to reanimate under whatever awful forces were responsible for this nightmare. One figure lay prone on the floor, his pants and underwear pooled around his ankles and head messily cleaved in half. It took Hutchinson a minute to figure out exactly what he was seeing and who the body had once belonged to.

"*Madre de dios*," Iglesias whispered, a hand covering her mouth.

Feminine laughter sounded through the hallway outside, and Hutchinson turned in time to see Coleridge's three daughters step into view.

"More toys," Diana said, smiling cruelly. Her flesh was so dry and cracked, her face looked like a broken desert landscape.

Iglesias screamed in pain as she flung her arm up, shockingly fast, and fired off two quick rounds. Diana and Christie Coleridge slumped to the ground, their mouths opened in Os of surprise, pus-colored eyes upturned toward the hole in each of their foreheads.

"Aww, that wasn't very nice," Evelyn, the president's prized daughter, said. She raised her fingers to her mouth to stifle her laughter.

"They ain't coming back, either, I don't think," Iglesias said.

"Nope, lights out for them," Evelyn said. "Daddy didn't like them much anyway, so not exactly a big loss, you know."

"Yeah, you always were his favorite, weren't you?" Hutchinson said.

Evelyn slowly raised the hem of her filthy skirt to her waist, revealing her naked and hairless sex. One inhumanly long, impossibly sharp claw slithered over her slit to collect the fluids pooling between her lean, muscular thighs. Then she raised that alien finger to her lips and sucked on it, waggling her eyebrows at Hutchinson. With her other hand, she used one bloody nail to pop loose the buttons of her blouse, her hard nipples poking at the fabric. "I am Daddy's little girl."

Iglesias shot her in the knee, and Evelyn's leg buckled, her weight sending her to the floor.

On the wall, beside the door, was an emergency fire axe and fire extinguisher. Hutchinson snatched the axe out of its cabinet and, in one fluid movement, brought it overhead as he turned. He slammed it down on Evelyn's wrist, and the force of the blow sent her deformed hand skittering across the floor, leaving a streak of blood.

The First Daughter's howls were bloodcurdling, and she lashed

out at him with her other hand. Iglesias stepped forward, pinning Evelyn's arm to the floor with her boot. Hutchinson took that hand off with another swing of the axe.

"Shoot her again," he said. "Just to be on the safe side."

Casually, Iglesias blew out Evelyn's other kneecap.

She tried to crawl on her elbows away from them, but Hutchinson planted a boot on her back. Pressing his Glock to one temple, he said to her, "I want answers."

"Fuck you." She spat blood at him but missed.

"Way I figure it, you're either going to bleed out, or I can shoot you in the head. Either way, you die, and you don't come back. Like your sisters there or Stephen or Melanie."

"Mom? You motherfucker!"

Evelyn screamed and tried to worm herself out from under Hutchinson's boot, but he stomped harder on her spine, turning her cries of anger into a shriek of pain.

"*Or*," he said, "you can live. We can get your bleeding under control, and maybe you live."

She kept fighting, until, eventually, she grew tired from the blood loss, and her head slumped to the floor.

"You can't stop it," she said.

"What is it? What is your father doing? *How* is he doing this?"

Hutchinson could tell she was out of it. Groggy and tired, she was fading fast.

"He died, you know," she said, her words coming in a slow slur. "It was all part of the plan. This is his country, and he's going to re-build it in his image. You can't stop him. This is his destiny. This was all part of the plan."

Her lips curled upward, and she began to laugh, pink bubbles popping along her chapped lips. Then her laughter slowed, and the

bubbles stop forming.

Hutchinson pressed his Glock tightly to her skull and pulled the trigger.

"We gotta find Coleridge," Iglesias said.

Standing, he gave her the once-over. Her body was clearly wracked with pain, and although she wouldn't tell him what exactly was wrong, she was in bad shape. Her complexion was sickly and pale, and she had difficulty moving. And when she did move, it cost her a lot.

"You sure you're up for it?"

She smirked. "I've been wanting to beat this pendejo's ass for four years, hermano. Let's go find him."

ELEVEN

ACTING PRESIDENT GRAHAM NEALY WATCHED on the plasma display screens as the world fell apart all around him. An hour ago, wildfires were surging in California, Black Lives Matter protestors were under attack by local factions of the 88 Blades white supremacist groups, and the police had attacked both. Now, all the news stations, national and local, had turned their eyes toward Washington, DC, and the White House. Despite the communications blackout, news had leaked anyway. He supposed it was inevitable, but he'd hoped for more time so they could better shape the narrative.

The narrative, such as it was, was predicated upon terrorism, but Coleridge, as usual, had turned even that simple, straightforward directive into a massive clusterfuck. The man had put himself right in the middle of the goddamn attack as its fucking ringleader! They'd been ready to blame Al-Qaeda or ISIS. Then those tweets—all those goddamned, motherfucking pre-scheduled and, now, delivered tweets—had gone out simultaneously from Coleridge and his family, all of them coordinated across multiple accounts to make for

one wholly unmistakable proclamation from the entire First Family. The words were seared into his retinas.

RETAKE the WHITE HOUSE for AMERICA!

The 88 Blades had responded in force, and now everything was back to being completely fucked again.

Fucking Coleridge. Nealy shoved a handful of pretzels into his mouth then washed it down with a tumbler of whiskey. *Why couldn't he just leave office like any other fucking normal human being?*

He ate and drank some more, mulling over what a fucking travesty of a human life Tyler Coleridge was. *Sore fucking goddamned degenerate fucking loser!*

Spoiled and stupid was a deadly combination, and Tyler Coleridge had been extreme in both measures. And that was just his public, outward persona! What the public didn't know, wasn't privy to, even despite all the various tell-all books written by former staffers, appointees to the White House, and even his own goddamned family was just how rotten and morally bankrupt Coleridge truly was on the inside. He showed the world some of that turpitude on a daily basis—but only some. Nealy doubted anybody could ever truly appreciate the fathoms of depravity that resided in Coleridge's soul, the darkness and rot that lived deep inside him.

He raised his tumbler and found it empty, so he refilled it for the fourth time.

United States Secret Service Director Barnes watched silently from the computer monitor. He was tucked into a window, beside Deputy Director Crouch and Chief Operating Officer Gavin. The triumvirate, they were the head of security, the men responsible for preventing any and all of this bullshit from ever happening. And they had just admitted to Nealy that they no longer had the ability to stop things on their own.

Nealy pinched the bridge of his nose and let out an exasperated breath. Then he shot back another finger's worth of whiskey.

"We are coordinating with DC Police, but our resources are stretched too thin. We've lost contact with the White House entirely, as well our agents stationed there, sir. Our own building is now under attack, and we've called in for all off-duty agents to respond. I think it's time we bring in the National Guard, Mr. Acting President."

Nealy turned his head and coughed into his elbow. It took him awhile to get it under control, and the sound of phlegm rattling in his chest was like crackers breaking. Red-faced and head swimming, he stood and nearly fell right back down into the seat.

He couldn't deal with this right now. He needed a moment to gather his thoughts, to calm down enough to make a logical, rational decision. The executive office was too small and hot, and the collar of his dress shirt was too tight. He loosened his tie and undid the top button, but that didn't make any of the pressure go away.

He popped more pretzels into his mouth, crunched them noisily, then shoved in another handful before he'd even swallowed the first one. His cheeks puffed out, and he gathered up more pretzels and his whiskey then put his back to the men on screen.

They called after him, but he ignored them. Unsteady on his feet, he shuffled into the bathroom, and, closing the door, popped in another pretzel, which he washed down with another slug of whiskey. Warmth flooded his belly and rode up his throat. He swallowed it down, along with a sizeable bite of pretzel.

The pretzel caught in his throat, a jagged point stabbing into either side of his esophagus. He coughed and tried to clear it out, but it stuck fast. His free hand went to his neck, trying to massage the blockage out of the way so he could breathe, but it was impossible

to budge. His lungs were burning, and he saw in the mirror how red his cheeks were becoming. His eyes were bulging from their sockets as he coughed and coughed and coughed.

Lightheaded, Nealy began to swoon. With the oxygen cut off from his brain, his knees weakened, and his vision dimmed. As he blacked out, on his way to the floor, his head cracked against the corner of the sink. He was dead before he slumped to the ground in front of the toilet.

A moment later, Nealy's hand reached up and grabbed the countertop. He hauled himself up and met his reflection in the mirror. He stared into his own yellow, mucus-colored eyes and smiled.

***

"What the hell do we do, Bob?" Director Barnes asked, turning to his deputy director.

Robert Crouch buried his face in the palms of his hands, feeling utterly defeated. He slicked back his hair, wishing for both a shower and whatever liquor cabinet Acting President Nealy had at hand. *I could use a good, stiff drink right about now. Or maybe two. Or ten. Ten would be good*, he thought, enough to send him into sweet, sweet oblivion.

"We need to bring in the Joint Chiefs and get the National Guard deployed. And we need Nealy on board."

"Well, we'll try again when he's out of the little boy's room." Barnes grunted.

Crouch was right there with him. They'd traded a psychotic for a limp-wristed weasel and at the worst time possible. Nealy was probably praying his way through a shit, and who knew how long that would take him? Things just kept going from bad to worse. Then,

right when he'd thought things couldn't get worse, worse had doubled down, and a fresh calamity washed over them.

At least Capitol Police had acted quickly to secure Congress. Most of the 535 members of the US Senate and the House of Representatives had been escorted out of the city. As a further precaution, Congressional leaders had been evacuated to a secure underground facility in order to, should the worst happen, ensure the continuity of the American government. Crouch desperately wanted to believe it was an overreaction, but these were unprecedented times, and he wasn't certain he could be sure of anything anymore.

He rubbed at his eyes, exhausted. The opening of a door behind them drew his attention, and he turned toward the entering agents, expecting some kind of update. More bad news, probably.

Instead of paperwork or digital tablets filling their hands, the agents carried only their guns.

"What is this?" Barnes snarled.

One agent turned toward him and said, "American exceptionalism." Then he fired, and Barnes's head snapped backward.

Crouch scrambled for his sidearm, but a second shot fired into his chest shoved him back in his chair. As he sat there, bleeding and fumbling for his gun, he got to watch, from a profile view, as the back of Gavin's skull exploded outward.

Another agent stepped forward, put the hot muzzle of his Glock to the center of Crouch's forehead, and pulled the trigger.

TWELVE

B Y 2001, TYLER COLERIDGE HAD already made his name and personal brand known globally. A brash businessman who had inherited millions of dollars from his father, he'd opened high-rise office towers, as well as casinos and various other businesses, all over the world with his name in giant gold letters right on their fronts. For a time, he'd had his own brand of pork and whiskey and even a fashion label. The darling of his portfolio, though, was the Miss Teen Galaxy beauty pageant. Every year, a new young lady between the ages of thirteen and nineteen was crowned as the loveliest and most astonishing and sophisticated girl in the Milky Way. And every year, Coleridge personally handpicked the winner.

That year, though, his life changed forever. Not in a monumental, all-at-once upheaval of personal good fortune, but through a series of events that would eventually escalate and coalesce with his becoming the president of the United States.

Russia had won the bid to host Miss Teen Galaxy 2001, giving Coleridge the chance not only to meet the Russian president, Mak-

sim Kuznetsov, but to dine and share the judges' tables with him. Kuznetsov was a surprisingly gracious host, and Coleridge admired his charm and proud bearing. The Russian president was young, fit, and strong, and if Coleridge were pressed, even he would have to admit he was smitten by the man. Kuznetsov had it all—a beautiful wife, beautiful daughters, and an incredible fortune that rivaled Coleridge's own. But more importantly, he had power and influence that exceeded anything Coleridge could imagine.

He'd heard the stories, of course, of how Kuznetsov was a thug, a mob boss who ran the Russian state like an organized crime outfit, and certainly, that was true. But it often overlooked the implications of what all that meant. It ignored the various state apparatuses that were at his disposal with intelligence, military services, and nuclear weaponry.

If pressed, Coleridge would deny it, but the truth was, he was envious. Almost exceptionally so. He wanted what Kuznetsov had.

Kuznetsov knew it too. He'd been able to read Coleridge like an open book and seemed able to look into the man's soul and pluck loose whatever information he so desired. That was when Kuznetsov had offered Coleridge that very same power. There was a catch, though, because of course there was.

Earlier that night, Coleridge had taken to the stage to crown a thirteen-year-old from Kentucky, her small breasts and hairless crotch barely concealed by the dental floss she called a string bikini. The state of her personal grooming was a fact known to Coleridge because earlier that evening, he had waltzed into the dressing room as the girls were preparing and had been delighted by a bevy of bare and scantily clad, nubile teenage flesh. After the show was over, he was invited to a private suite at the Hyatt. He would be joined there by Kuznetsov and several other guests. Even though the recently sec-

ond-time divorced billionaire wanted to do little more that evening than congratulate the Kentucky winner in his own special and private way back at his own suite, turning down the Russian president's invitation was simply impossible.

He rode in Kuznetsov's limousine. Massive SUVs with darkened windows flanked the vehicle, and several more led and followed the limo to the Hyatt. Coleridge and Kuznetsov made small talk and drank whiskey, which Kuznetsov preferred over vodka. Charming as always, he was sure to let Coleridge know what a wonderful distillery the man was operating. Whatever else they talked about, Coleridge forgot. So much of the evening was a blur, except for what came after they arrived at Kuznetsov's private presidential suite at the Moscow Hyatt.

Coleridge was led inside, where he was introduced to a number of businessmen and their wives, girlfriends, or trophies who clung to them. Among them was Melanie Sidorov, one of the most popular and sexiest models in Russia and a personal friend to Kuznetsov's family. She had a thick mane of blond hair, and her irises were so blue, they looked like the ocean itself had been trapped in her eyes, flecked with golden chips of sunlight. Instead of shaking his hand, Melanie leaned in and greeted him with a kiss to the cheek, lingering longer than she had to.

Kuznetsov whispered in his ear, "She's single," and bumped his arm with his elbow, smiling knowingly.

A massive television was tuned to the state-owned news network, Russia Now. Two empty plush chairs were arranged before the TV. Kuznetsov took one and invited Coleridge to take the other, then the younger man took up a chunky remote and pressed some buttons. The screen changed, and Coleridge instantly lost all color.

The monitor now showed a split-screen broadcast that provided

a three-hundred-sixty-degree field of coverage from multiple angles. The clarity of the recordings from the hidden cameras was startlingly clear, and in the center of the screen was Tyler Coleridge himself, naked and spread-eagle atop a king-size bed. Rope bound each of his limbs to the four posters of the bedframe.

He was not alone, though. With him were a trio of young girls, all naked. Anyone who had watched that evening's Miss Teen Galaxy would recognize them as contestants from France, Russia, and Italy.

The fourteen-year-old from France was squatting above Coleridge's face, her feet planted on either side of his head. She had to hold on to the headboard for support. The hidden camera zoomed in for a closer look, and Coleridge could feel the weight of all the eyes upon him as he watched the child urinate on his face. TV Coleridge sputtered, spitting piss out of his mouth, then licked his lips.

"Mmm, baby," his tinny voice said through the television, "you've been drinking coffee, haven't you? You smell like coffee."

On screen, his small cock trembled and hardened. Then the fifteen-year-old from Italy took her turn, a thick, dark-yellow spray geysering from between her legs to wash over Coleridge's face and hair. A dark stain spread across his bedsheets, and again, he spit and heaved in air, as if he'd just been waterboarded.

In the Hyatt, he shifted uncomfortably in the chair. He tried to stand, but a vise-like hand squeezed his shoulder painfully hard and pushed him back down. His wide ass sank into the soft cushion, and the hand stayed there a moment. Coleridge looked at Kuznetsov, but the man, his face placid, merely watched the television, his legs crossed, and sipped at his tumbler of whiskey.

Coleridge opened his mouth to speak. That hand applied pressure to his shoulder again, and he felt his collarbone creak and threaten to break. His jaws snapped closed. He wanted to close his eyes in

The Russian girl was crying as she dismounted the bed, and Coleridge lay, content, in a foul puddle of waste. The other two girls stood dumbly beside the bed, ill looks on their faces, and clearly unsure what to do next. They exchanged uncomfortable and embarrassed glances with one another. After a moment of uncertainty, they traded turns in the bathroom to clean themselves and get dressed, and one of them loosened the knots. They left Coleridge as he was— snoring loudly, asleep in their filth.

Finally, Kuznetsov pressed a button to stop the tape and turned off the television. He turned his body in the chair to face Coleridge more directly, holding his empty tumbler against one knee. "You work for me now, *da*."

***

As the night wore on, Coleridge spent much of it feeling drunk and dizzy. He knew there would be no rebelling against Kuznetsov. To do so would be the end of his own empire and ambitions. The more Kuznetsov explained about the benefits of their relationship, though, the less Coleridge wanted to part ways. The Russian president shared with him a vision and a plan. Then he introduced Melanie's older brother, Sergey, who was a psychic.

In the years following the collapse of the Soviet Union, Russians had begun seeking new beliefs and ideologies to replace the tenants of Communism, and Sergey Sidorov had earned himself a devout following after a televised faith healing in the late 1980s. The man had cured cripples on live television in a Kremlin-approved broadcast then performed psychic readings to reconnect audience members with their dead loved ones. Coleridge's first instinct was to brush it off as little more than con artistry, a field he knew quite well after all

his years in business, and dismiss the psychic as nothing more than some second-rate John Edward/David Copperfield rip-off. Sergey's proclamations, however, were rather endearing and specific, and so Coleridge was willing to entertain the man.

"You will become president of the United States," Sergey had told him, his cool, steely eyes boring into Coleridge's as he gripped both hands in his. "And you will make my wife an American princess."

Sergey smiled widely at this particular prognostication and looked toward Melanie, clearly proud. Her face was stony and bored looking, a far cry from the wild, sexy smile she wore on so many magazine covers the world over, but she nodded in acknowledgement.

Sergey turned Coleridge's hands over, palm-side up. Then he nodded toward President Kuznetsov and, again, at Melanie. "He is ready to accept his gift now, I believe."

Kuznetsov and Melanie stepped over the thick line of salt that had been poured in a wide circle across the floor. Inside the circle, more lines of salt formed a large pentagram, with additional strange-looking markings made between the five points of the star. They joined Sergey and Coleridge inside the large pentagon at the heart of the occult symbol and made a circle with their bodies.

From the inside pocket of his suit jacket, Kuznetsov removed a switchblade and flicked open the knife. He made a shallow cut along Coleridge's palm, following the man's lifeline with the blade, then did the same to his own then Melanie's and Sergey's. Blood dripped from their palms and splattered onto the carpet between them.

Dressed in thick wool robes and holding hands, the other attendants of Kuznetsov's gathering stood around the salt circle. They began to chant, then, more loudly, Sergey began to speak. Although

Coleridge didn't understand any of the words, he knew the psychic wasn't speaking Russian. There was a different tenor, a different flavor, to the foreign words.

Stranger, still, was the acrid smell permeating the suite. It was rich, heady, and intoxicating. Coleridge breathed deeply of the dark, earthy scent. The room smelled of spice and decay, a conflicting aroma of pleasantry and rot that was oddly soothing. As he soaked in the dank scent and the hum of chanting voices—some loud, some soft—he felt a lightness enter his being. Then he began to relax as his muscles loosened.

Slowly, he began to realize that at some point, Kuznetsov and Sergey had let go of his hands, and he was left alone in the heart of the pentagram with only Melanie, both of her hands in his. She stepped forward, toe-to-toe with him, and pressed her lips to his. Her tongue slipped between his teeth, and he pulled her tightly to his body, his dick hardening against her belly. Her hands fumbled for his belt then undid the button and fly of his trousers while he hiked up her skirt and yanked down her underwear.

Careful not to break the lines of salt, they shimmied out of their clothes and lay down in the center of the pentagon. Melanie straddled Coleridge's hips and, reaching behind herself, guided him into her. The chanting of the cloaked men and women gathered around them grew louder and more insistent as Melanie impaled herself upon Coleridge's cock. The words became stronger and more urgent as she rode him to his climax.

Their marriage consummated in the center of this pentagram, she pulled herself away from her husband's rapidly shriveling member and found her clothes. Coleridge slowly got to his feet and dressed, the chanting having stopped. Candles were being extinguished as he dressed.

Sergey approached him with an extended hand. "She will learn to love you in time," he said. These words were the first hint of dishonesty Coleridge had detected from the man the entire night. Kuznetsov handed him a fresh tumbler of whiskey.

"Who needs her heart when you have her pussy, da?" He laughed, and they clinked glasses.

"Either way," Sergey said, "she will give you a daughter who is loyal to you, who will do *anything* for you."

Coleridge considered Sergey's words, nodding slowly. "Now what?" he asked, savoring the cold burn of the whiskey as it washed down his throat and into his belly.

"Now," Kuznetsov said, smirking and with a raised eyebrow, "you enjoy your honeymoon. We will handle the rest."

***

Kuznetsov delivered on his promises. In the years that followed his return to the US with his new bride, Tyler Coleridge's star rose and rose. His businesses became more profitable, due in no small part to the Russian mob money being laundered through his casinos in New Jersey and Detroit. He became a staple on Fox News, regularly appearing on their morning show and evening business news programming. In 2003, NBC approached him to host a reality television series centered around turning C- and D-list celebrities the public had forgotten into CEOs of various Coleridge-brand businesses.

Coleridge's celebrity and financial cachet grew and grew, and for ten years, his reality show dominated prime time. Week after week, he uttered his catchphrase—"You're outta here!"—to dismiss the failed celebrities, delivering it like the world's angriest, most put-up-on baseball umpire there ever was. It became a brand unto itself,

repeated in households across the country. His show was particularly big in the Midwest, and even kids began dressing like him for Halloween, wearing sneering orange plastic masks that, like a recognizable caricature, bore only a passing resemblance to him.

Then, in 2015, he met with a team of Russians sent on behalf of Kuznetsov in his New York penthouse. It was time, Kuznetsov said via an encrypted satellite phone, that he began getting ready for his presidential bid. Kuznetsov's aides then introduced Coleridge to the men who would be managing his campaign.

Paperwork was filed. Then, as he and Melanie descended a golden escalator into the heart of the lobby of Coleridge Tower, Coleridge made his announcement to the media: he was running as a Republican candidate for the office of president of the United States of America. Wearing a bright-red baseball hat bearing the words American Exceptionalism, he said to the throng of reporters, "We're gonna remember what it means to be an American."

"Look at this country. Look at what it's become, people," Coleridge said, affecting an air of sadness and disappointment as he looked around at each journalist and camera operator. "This country is trash. You know that? It's absolute trash. No, no, no, don't look at me like that. You know what I'm saying is true. This country is trash, and you know it. But do you know why? I'll tell you why! We're letting in so many immigrants these days, so many. So, so many."

His voice grew more and more heated as he went on. "All these Mexicans coming in across the border, sending their drugs into our ports and piers and tunnels, all these rapists and killers coming here. That's what they all are, you know. All these Mexicans? They're killers, folks. Killers and rapists, and they're coming after you, coming for your kids by hook or by crook, I promise you. If they can't catch your kids and gut 'em in an alley, they'll get 'em with their needles,

'cause that's why they're all here. They're destroying our country—you know that's true! You know that's true. And the fags—don't even get me started, all right?

"I'm not saying anything you don't already know. But what I'm gonna do, it's gonna be so good. So beautiful. It's going to be *tremendous*. And it's so simple, what I'm gonna do. You know what I'm going to do? For you, my fellow Americans, all you hard workers out there wanting a piece of that sweet, sweet American Dream but instead are watching all these Mexicans and Pakistanis taking it from you. What I'm gonna do is, I'm gonna fix it. That's all. It's time to send a message to these Washington elites, these Ivy League know-nothings and do-nothings. What have they ever done for you, huh? Other than take and take and take? I'm not like them, people."

Coleridge took off his red hat for a brief moment and swept his hair back. He paused to take a drink of water, meeting the eyes of the people before him. He smiled, leaning against the podium, and kept the audience in suspense for a brief moment. When he spoke again, it was with fiery conviction, his personality shifting from a wealthy businessman living in a golden tower to that of a preacher at a revival, commanding everyone's attention.

"I am going to make this country beautiful again. So, so beautiful. You can count on that. We're going to put up a wall, and we're going to stop these illegal Mexicans from ruining this fine country any further, and if that doesn't work, we're going to nuke them back to the stone age, okay? And I know, I know, they're pretty much already stuck in the Stone Age, aren't they? Bunch of poor, filthy, old slobs down there, aren't they? They're backwards. Backwards. It's a shame, but it's true. They are. They are. And we're gonna round up all these Mexicans, all these A-rabs that are here illegally, these spics and these ragheads, and you know what we're gonna say to them?

When we round them up? You know what we're gonna say? I bet you do. I bet you do!"

And here, he pumped his fist in the air, thumb out, and cocked it back over his shoulder in dramatic fashion. "You're outta here!"

The journalists exchanged looks, partly worried and partly amused by what they thought was the absolute and willful destruction of one man's career on live TV. The audience assembled in the lobby that day, though? They loved it, and Coleridge's words were met with thunderous applause and loud, echoing cheers.

The rest was history.

***

Over the course of the last half of 2015 and right up until election day of the following year, Coleridge held one rally after another all across the country, hitting up each and every state. His group of supporters grew larger and larger with each magnanimous boast, and they clapped, hooted, and hollered at every one of his racist antics. He attacked reporters, minorities, and elected officials. He verbally assaulted the military, the nation's intelligence agents, and law enforcement. And the American people loved him for it. They claimed the rich, elite New York loudmouth as one of their own.

"He talks just like us," his supporters claimed. After Coleridge spent one rowdy rally mocking the disabled and demanding the Black protestors be beaten by those members of 88 Blades in attendance, those interviewed happily responded, "He's one of us!"

Every poll said it was impossible for Coleridge to win. Every pundit promised the world that America was better than this, swearing that it would be impossible for Coleridge to secure his party's nomination. Then, after he did, they assured the public that Coleridge's

winning the election wasn't in the cards. Even his chosen party wrote him off as an aberration. When asked about Coleridge's chances in the lead-up to the primary, one sitting GOP senator told reporters that if Coleridge won the nomination, their party was doomed.

Coleridge never doubted his imminent victory. He had no reason to. He could feel it in his bones. Never had there been any self-doubt. Never did his confidence diminish. He was going to win, and he was going to become the most powerful man on earth.

After news broke that, eleven years earlier, Coleridge had been in his New York penthouse with three prostitutes while Melanie was giving birth to Maddock, the Christians who'd flocked to his side praised him as a gift from God and proof of the Heavenly Father's glory. Evangelicals worshipped at the altar of Tyler Coleridge in the fervent hope that this man had been handpicked by God Almighty to, at last, bring about Biblical Armageddon and fulfill the apocalyptic prophecies written within the Book of Revelation.

It wasn't God who had helped Coleridge ascend to the most powerful office in the world, though. Although he wasn't a believer in any deity, he couldn't help but find some measure of faith as his margin for electoral college victory grew wider and wider. He began to believe that Kuznetsov's beliefs and the ceremonies he had half-heartedly taken part in over the last fifteen years had, in fact, been legitimate.

Kuznetsov had promised to take care of everything, and Coleridge believed that he had. But not without help. Coleridge's victory had been blessed by a higher power.

The Russian president was a fervent Molochian, and his faith had rubbed off on Coleridge. Melanie, too, was a believer, as was her brother, Sergey. Coleridge had never had much interest in religion, and he'd turned a blind eye as Melanie raised Maddock in her

faith and even converted Evelyn. Over the last decade, as Coleridge further enmeshed his older sons and daughters in his various business interests and network of contacts, they, too, had become devout Molochians and believers in the fruit that was being delivered unto them by their new god.

As the clock ticked over from November eighth, Election Day, to November ninth, Coleridge finally accepted the truth of it all. Moloch was his savior, and all that he now possessed was because his god had granted him favor. He was the wealthiest American alive, a television star, husband to a glamorous model, father to a big-titted Barbie doll of a girl, and now, he was president of the United States. All of the public boasting he'd made about having built all of wealth himself, he had to admit, was nothing more than theater. What he had now, Moloch had given him, and he would be forever indebted to Maksim Kuznetsov for inducting him into the cabal.

But Kuznetsov wanted more. The Russian president was the first foreign dignitary to visit the White House. Shaking hands with Kuznetsov before the press, Coleridge promised America that Russia was their friend and that the allegations of Russian interference in the election was nothing more than a hoax perpetrated by the liberals. Kuznetsov stayed for four days, and for three nights, the men stayed up late, drinking whiskey in the living room on the second floor of the White House residence.

Kuznetsov never had to mention the tape to Coleridge. Both men knew what was on it and that Kuznetsov possessed it and could release it whenever he wanted. It was an invisible guillotine blade that constantly hung above Coleridge's head. If that tape documenting his perversions with a trio of teenage girls and the fetishes he'd engaged in with them were ever to be leaked to the press, he would be ruined instantaneously. His political career would be over. He

would never be allowed on television ever again. He might even end up in prison.

They clinked their glasses together and drank. "Praise Moloch," Kuznetsov said softly, and Coleridge repeated the oath. In the hours that followed, they discussed their plans for the next four years and how Coleridge would use his time in office to not only strengthen his own business interests and further pad his offshore bank accounts but to also enhance Kuznetsov's own network of criminal enterprises.

Coleridge would spend the next four years destabilizing and weakening every institution of American government that he could, to the point of collapse if possible, all the while continuing to hold his rallies and remind his supporters of his strengths, to remind them to hate, and to sow divisions between their families and neighbors.

For Moloch. But also for myself, he had to admit. He knew his god of war would understand, for both of them reveled in the power of hatred. The ancient Canaanite deity was a god of child sacrifice through fire and war, and Coleridge was intent on delivering his offerings.

With each rally he held, parents cut ties with their children as their hearts hardened and hate was allowed to consume their souls. Wildfires exploded across the western seaboard, and he let them burn uncontrolled as the skies turned orange and rained ash upon the people, flames eating their homes and burning to death hundreds. Anti-fascist protestors clashed violently in the streets with the combined forces of police and local 88 Blades chapters, as well as the other neo-Nazi and Aryan Brotherhood gangs that flew Coleridge flags and wore Coleridge hats. A deadly virus swept across the globe, infecting and killing millions, and he used federal law enforcement agencies to seize ventilators and personal protective equipment from state health agencies and hospitals, to stockpile for his own use in

the coming years, and openly encouraged Americans to defy Centers for Disease Control guidelines to wear face coverings to protect themselves and others. He stoked the flames for violence even higher, taking to his Twitter account and encouraging his supporters to overthrow government officials who encouraged quarantine lockdowns to slow and contain the spreading pandemic, setting up further clashes between protestors, counter-protestors, and the police as the 88 Blades and armed militia members proudly bearing the Confederate flag stormed their state capitol buildings and openly threatened lawmakers.

He watched while fear engulfed the country as Americans burned, rioted, and died by the hundreds of thousands. For Moloch.

And then his bid for reelection came due. The race was tighter than he had expected. For all the souls he had twisted and maligned in Moloch's name, it hadn't been enough to secure a victory. Granted, seventy-four million Americans wanted to keep fighting and sacrificing, to continue stewing in hate and destruction, and to raze and salt the earth they lived on. That was a victory in its own right. His base of supporters had grown even larger over his four years of wrath and destruction. He knew Moloch would be proud and that his dark god had grown so much stronger during his first term as president. He had done as his god, and as Kuznetsov, had demanded of him.

His reward was within reach. All it required was a little more sacrifice. Sacrifice on a much grander scale.

***

Coleridge led David through the lobby of the West Wing, down a stairwell, and into the basement. From there, he followed a corridor to what looked like a freight elevator. His cabinet would have been

evacuated to the Deep Underground Command Center, he knew, and that was where he would find Secretary of State Nicholas Furth and the metal Zero Halliburton briefcase known as "the football."

He wiped his stained hand on his pants and willed his hand to relax back into its smaller, more-human configuration. The transformation was painful, as bone ground against bone and skin knitted back together. When it was finished, his hand looked swollen and black, as if it had sustained serious trauma. He pressed his palm to the electronic scanner beside the elevator doors and watched the screen change from black to green.

A hushed rumbling noise grew from behind the walls, and a moment later, the doors parted to reveal a spacious metal car. Inside was a four-man squad of Army soldiers ready for battle.

Coleridge's hand stretched painfully, bony claws exploding through fattened fingers, and he leapt forward. The soldiers opened fire, their 5.56x45mm NATO rounds ripping through the president's chest and belly and into his son's torso.

Being shot hurt, but Coleridge had grown accustomed to pain. He found the noise more bothersome, and with his large claws, he tore away their machine guns and tossed the weaponry aside.

"Not the heads," he said to David.

His son smiled, revealing thick white fangs.

"Attaboy."

The elevator doors shut behind them, trapping the screams of the soldiers inside. David's teeth sank into one man's throat, while Coleridge thrust his dagger-like fingers into the soft, unprotected tissues of another man's crotch. His nails glided over the man's femoral artery, and the soldier bled out within moments while Coleridge ripped open the throat of a second soldier.

David licked the gore from his lips.

"Bunch of losers," Coleridge said, looking at the dead Army men. "But you'll thank me later."

He turned to the elevator's control panel and pressed the button to lower the car to the base of its shaft, two thousand feet below.

More soldiers were waiting for them when the doors opened.

THIRTEEN

Hutchinson's phone vibrated in his pocket. It had been doing that on and off all night, but with the crisis unfolding all around him, he'd been forced to ignore it. Even without looking at it, he knew who it was. He also knew he might not have another chance to answer, and he hated the idea of dying without the chance to speak to his son one last time.

"I need to take this," he said to Iglesias, pulling his phone free. The violence of this long night had left the screen spiderwebbed with cracks, but the device still appeared functional enough.

She quirked an eyebrow at him, but he ignored it and turned away from her. Pressing his back to the wall, he took a quick look at the home screen. He had just missed this latest call, but the phone lit up with a notification of seven other missed calls. He watched as the seven rolled to an eight, all from the same phone number. There were a dozen text message alerts from the same number, as well. He saw "Are you okay?" and "I love you" as he hit the call back button.

Robbie answered immediately, his ten-year-old voice shrieking into the phone. "Oh my God, Dad! Are you okay? Mom's had the news on all night."

"Hey, buddy. Yeah, I'm fine. Things are just…" He laughed. *How to even describe this fucking nightmare?* "Things are weird and crazy."

"I saw Coleridge yelling at that reporter. Did you get to hit him?"

Hutchinson couldn't help but laugh again. "No, no, son. Sorry."

There were few things his son wanted to see more than his old man deck the president, except maybe some real-life dinosaurs. It was a thought that broke Hutchinson's heart, the ways in which Coleridge and his administration had so thoroughly poisoned this country and its citizens with its constant lies and assaults on the norms of basic human decency and morality.

Robbie had several Latinx friends at school and on his softball team, and although they were second- and third-generation Americans, the boy had once shared his fears with his father. He worried his friends would be taken by the president and locked up in cages simply for being brown-skinned, and he'd even had a nightmare or two about such an awful scenario. It was a terrible thing for a child to have to confront such baseless evil at so early an age. Robbie knew it was perhaps an unreasonable fear, but what really killed Hutchinson was that there now existed an entire generation of children and young Americans, hell, even a lot of adults for that matter, for whom the office holder of president of the United States was a boogeyman.

"What's the news saying?" Hutchinson asked.

"Shit's out of control," Robbie said, then a moment later added, "Sorry."

"It's okay. It's also not wrong."

"There's protests breaking out everywhere. Cops are losing it. What, um, what's happening there? Is it really as bad as they're saying?"

"What are they saying?"

"There's news copters flying over DC and…" Robbie's voice

162

hitched. "They're calling it a bloodbath, Dad."

"They're not wrong. But look, buddy. Maybe it's not such a good idea for you to be watching this stuff."

"Yeah, that's what Mom said. She sent me to my room, but it's all over the internet. Everyone on Facebook and Twitter is talking about it."

"I thought I said no social media for you."

"Mom said it was okay…"

Goddamn it, Alicia. "Well, I guess it's too late now."

"It's like something out of a movie," Robbie said. "The news, they're saying people are coming back from the dead. That can't happen, though, can it?"

"I don't know what's happening," Hutchinson said. Alicia, his ex-wife, was going to have her hands full tonight, dealing with Robbie's nightmares. "Just stay inside, okay? You and your mom. Keep the doors and windows locked. You got that?"

"Yeah, we're not going anywhere."

"These people that are coming back. Is that just in DC?"

"It's all over, Dad. I mean, like, everywhere. New York, Philly, Oregon, California. All over the place. Cops are shooting protestors, those weirdo racists are killing both sides, but nobody's staying down. It's nuts."

What the hell has Coleridge done?

Hutchinson swallowed a lump in his throat, his mouth dry. "Look, bud, I have to go. We've got to take care of some stuff here. I don't know when I'll be able to talk again. I love you, pal."

"I love you, too, Dad."

The phone went dead. Tears stung Hutchinson's eyes, and he wiped them away with the back of his hand. He felt sick.

"You all right?" Iglesias asked, putting a hand on his shoulder.

Awkwardly, she gave him a hug then thumped his back, wincing as she did so.

He took a deep breath and tried to center his thoughts. "I'm good," he said, but his voice was shaky and not the least bit convincing. "I'm good," he said, this time with more steel.

The only signs of Coleridge and his son were the filthy footprints the two had left behind on their rampage through the West Wing. Hutchison and Iglesias followed the stains to the stairs heading to the basement, and Hutchinson realized where Coleridge was going with a sinking feeling. Acid burbled in his stomach, and bile rose.

The Deep Underground Command Center, four thousand feet below the White House, where the last vestiges of this administration were sheltering away from all this madness. Coleridge was going to them, and the implications sent a wave of fear through Hutchinson. He thought also of Colette and tried his best to send positive vibes to her. She was a strong woman, a fighter, and proficient agent, as evidenced by her place at the head of the vice president's protective detail. She could handle whatever came her way.

When this was all over, he looked forward to seeing her smile again, the way joy lit up her eyes and crinkled the soft brown skin around each orb. It was an infectious smile, and he couldn't help but smile in turn as he thought of how her face brightened.

She is going to make it, he thought. *Whatever happens, she's going to be just fine.* Coleridge didn't know what he was up against with her.

"C'mon," Iglesias said. "Let's get going."

Hutchinson nodded, and he walked beside the sniper as they wound their way down the stairwell, following bloody footprints to a large freight elevator.

***

Hutchinson had to turn his face away from the stench that boiled out of the freight car as the elevator doors slid open. A coppery, metallic stink turned the air leaden, and beneath that rancorous odor was a deeper, rotten smell. The freight car itself was filthy, its walls painted in blood and chunks of flesh. Flies alighted from the gobs of meat strewn across each of the cube's surfaces, the noise of their buzzing terribly loud in the enclosed space, and circled around him and Iglesias.

They had no choice but to step into the filth. Iglesias gagged into the crook of her elbow as she tried to cover her face.

Hutchinson was grateful for the nonslip treads of his oxfords. The black shoes looked dressy and complimented the pinstripe suit he wore, but they were much more comfortable than dress shoes and were ideal for security work. They also kept him standing as he navigated the slippery floor.

He kept his lips parted slightly to breathe through his mouth, not wanting to offer a fresh opening for the flies to explore. His eyes were drawn to one of the bullet holes pockmarking the walls, and he watched as a large blowfly emerged from the cavity. The smell of death was pungent enough that he could practically taste the gore and excrement surrounding him. He couldn't help but notice that, despite the mess, there were no bodies.

Although he had already done so earlier, he again checked the H&K MP-5 submachine gun to ensure a round was chambered and that the forty-round extended magazine was fully loaded. Strapped crosswise across his body, the weapon hung at his side while he checked his Glock 19 then holstered the sidearm at his hip. Prior to exiting the ground floor of the West Wing, he and Iglesias had replenished supplies at the Secret Service Command Center and now

had dozens of extra magazines for the guns they carried scattered between their various pockets of their tactical chest rigs and pants. Iglesias had opted for the SR-16 CQB assault rifle favored by the agents in the Counter Assault Team.

Hutchinson was exhausted and jittery. Scared too. But he also felt, if not exactly prepared, then at least *ready*. He knew what was waiting for them, in theory at least, if not how many. He wasn't delusional about his odds of survival either. His training, preparedness, reflexes, and more than his own fair share of good luck had kept him alive thus far, but he didn't know how much longer they would see him through the night.

He shuddered at the thought of what was waiting for them as the elevator descended, then he pushed those dark ideas away. He tried to focus on Robbie instead. His cell phone would be useless in the DUCC, and he was grateful he'd had a chance to talk to his boy before entering the elevator. It had been a welcome break from the madness.

With his rotating work schedule, it had been hard to find the time to actually see Robbie outside of FaceTime, let alone spend a day with his boy. Working for the Secret Service meant Hutchinson had absolutely no work-life balance at all, and he was constantly at the mercy of the job. It was one of the factors that had led to his divorce, and Alicia had, rightly and more than once, accused him of never being there for them. He didn't have a fixed nine-to-five with weekends off. His scheduled days off continuously changed, and he usually didn't know what the following week's schedule would look like until the Friday before. In some ways, it reminded him of when he'd worked retail to help pay his way through college. To add to the stress, there was the almost constant travel, with little to no notice at all. Under Coleridge's presidency, Hutchinson found himself more

often at one of the president's golf resorts than at home.

He hadn't been oblivious to the strain his work had placed on his relationship with Alicia. Every time she pointed out how difficult making their marriage work was, he'd sympathized. His heart ached for every Christmas, Thanksgiving, and birthday he'd missed with her and Robbie, but he'd also been unwilling to sacrifice his job for his family. He loved his work, and for the last decade, he'd been living out his childhood dream.

Alicia wasn't. She'd always wanted to have a family, with a husband who was there for her. What she'd gotten instead was raising a child practically all on her own. She had a regular job and pulled double duty as a parent.

When she'd told him a few years ago that she'd been seeing another man, he'd almost felt relieved. A part of him had even been happy for her. It had dawned on him then that he knew more about what was happening in the lives of the agents he worked with than what was happening under his own roof. He hadn't argued when she asked for a divorce and sole custody of Robbie. Moving out of their home had been one of the toughest moments of his life, and holding on to his son as Robbie cried against his chest had left permanent scars slashed across his heart.

He'd been selfish. He'd taken his wife for granted. Now, he wondered if he would ever see either of them again. If not, at least he had made sure his son knew his father loved him. If the last words Robbie ever remembered Hutchinson sharing with him were those, at least they were good ones.

Iglesias was staring at him, concerned. He took a deep breath and cleared his mind.

"You got anybody waiting at home for you, Iglesias?"

Slowly, she shook her head. "Nah. Mom and Dad, they died

when I was young. Pretty much was raised in the foster system then enlisted when I hit eighteen." She shrugged, a coy smile on her lips. "Some ladies I wouldn't mind seeing again if we make it through this, but other than that… It's just me and my cat, and my neighbor pretty much already takes care of that mangy old thing for me anyway."

He let out a small laugh. "What kind of cat?"

"A seventeen-year-old calico. Freddy. Love that guy." She fished for her cell phone and opened the photos app.

He laughed easier at the photo she'd captured of Freddy in midyawn, his eyes pinched shut. "Cute."

"He's a sweetie." Like a proud mother sharing pictures of her newborn, she swiped through a few more then tucked the phone away, wincing at the pain moving brought her. "Christ, my back. I got this chair, most comfortable thing in the world, you know? Gonna sit my ass down, pull on a nice fleece blanket, and Freddy, he's gonna jump up in my lap and sit with me and give me *all* the cuddles."

She shook her head as if in wonder. "Cats, man. They're good for the soul. You got pets?"

"No, I don't."

"Pets're better than people. You should get one."

Hutchinson had had a dog growing up, but with his schedule, he didn't want to put an animal's life in his hands. Colette had talked about getting a cat, though, and he thought that might be kind of nice. She understood the job, its demands, and its meaning. She got it, and that helped smooth over some of those rougher bumps in a relationship.

"Maybe one day," he said.

The elevator slowed and eased to a stop. Its doors parted.

Hutchinson and Iglesias traded glances and raised their weapons. Then they stepped into hell.

FOURTEEN

LONG BEFORE HE'D BECOME PRESIDENT, Tyler Coleridge had been a fan of the military tactic known as shock and awe. It was a practice he'd applied to his business affairs and something he'd routinely used over the course of his campaign for presidency and his time in office. On the campaign trail, he'd lobbed off lies upon lies as if they were cruise missiles and built entire speeches on exaggerations and falsehoods, distracting journalists and fact checkers who raced to correct his claims, while ignoring the substantive central messages of his campaign.

Upon capturing the Oval Office, one of his first orders of business had been to issue a flurry of executive orders in a rapid, scatter-shot assault that journalists, the public, and even other government officials found impossible to keep up with. The aim had been to cow and rattle Congress and bring them to heel for his own desires. Only two weeks after being sworn in, he'd single-handedly shut down America's refugee program, blocked visas to Muslims, banned travelers from more than half a dozen Arab countries, promised to publish

weekly lists of crimes committed by immigrants, expanded the powers and scope of ICE, broadened the definitions of who was subject to deportation, and eliminated health care and employment protections for transgender, homosexual, and disabled Americans. He'd also authorized the forced separation of families captured illegally crossing the Mexican border into the United States and arranged for the establishment of concentration camps along the border to imprison detainees. He'd allowed for tear gas to be fired over the border, even though the practice violated international chemical weapons bans and international human rights standards, including Article 2 of the United Nations Charter, which the United States had signed.

The overriding message to the people, their representatives, the press, and the world over was simple and concise: *I can do whatever I want, and you can't stop me.*

That message had all but defined Coleridge's entire life and his singular motivations in the pursuit for power. He was rich and popular, and thusly the world was his for the taking. Any attempt to stop him was carried out at the naysayer's own peril.

Even now, people were trying to stop him and were failing. He'd left a trail of bodies in his wake, and blood pooled along the floor from one end of the Executive Office to the other.

On the monitors arrayed around the room, he watched, with an erection growing in his pants, as chaos unfolded across the US. The national news outlets had broken their individual broadcasts into split-screen narratives to showcase the rioting and looting happening all across America. At the center of each, though, was the White House, where armies of the dead were amassing to claim the lives of others. The anchors were scrambling to find scientists and doctors who could explain what was happening as they likened it to a zombie outbreak. As usual, they were wrong. *Fake news, all of it.*

The Evangelicals, though, the ones shouting and flailing about the demonic takeover of America, were closer to the truth.

At every rally and campaign stop Coleridge had made over the last five years, Melanie had been with him, offstage, behind the scenes, working her magic and opening doors for him into the hearts and minds of the American people. With each ticket sold to one of his events, the attendees had been selling their souls wholesale without even knowing it, their bodies waiting for the final piece of the ritual to fall into place—Coleridge's own death and the consecration of a deal made with a devil.

After his return and in the chaos that had followed, Melanie had been free to work her magic and finalize the terms that would unleash hell on earth. The barriers between life and death were shattered, and the gates to hell were flung wide open. Each human death left a free skinsuit ripe for habitation by long-waiting demons that were now free.

Melanie's death had tidily solved the question of what to do with her once she'd served her purposes. Also handily resolved was Nealy's demise. The creature wearing Nealy's cracked and pale skin was certainly a far more faithful servant than the insufferably Christian lackey had once been. Rather than argue for Coleridge's place in heaven, the Nealy-thing had helped to secure his military aide and Secretary of Defense Nicholas Furth.

On the polished oak table at the center of the room sat a large black briefcase that weighed roughly forty-five pounds. Inside it was a laptop computer, the Black Book containing nuclear strike retaliatory options printed in red on black pages, a book listing classified site locations around the country, where the president could be taken in an emergency, a manila folder containing procedures on how to operate the Emergency Broadcast System, and a three-by-five-inch

card with authentication codes to order the launch of nuclear weapons. The codes were of the most interest to President Coleridge.

Seated at the table were Nealy's aide and Secretary of Defense Furth. Standing directly behind them were Nealy and David Coleridge.

The men were facing a group of monitors. On one pair of screens were various news outlets broadcasting the violence taking place across the nation above. On another monitor were the pensive faces of Coleridge's Joint Chiefs of Staff, broadcasting from their meeting room in the Pentagon. The Joint Chiefs watched silently as Nealy's military aide unbuckled the Zero Halliburton briefcase and removed the EMP shielded and hardened, drop-proof computer. Nealy's prodigious claws encircled the aide's neck. Sweating, the man began to input his security access codes. The laptop's embedded camera scanned the aide's retina, and the computer unlocked.

"Please, sir, we are asking you, again, to reconsider." This came from the Chairman of the Joint Chiefs of Staff, General Brian Cutter, United States Army. He looked as pale as the rest of the men—six generals from the army, air force, space force, marine corps, and one admiral from the navy. A few minutes ago, Coleridge had informed each of them that their families had been taken into custody and transferred to secure locations but that their safety could not be guaranteed. They were then allowed to access a link to a website that showed them their family members in captivity and being guarded by members of the 88 Blades. To hammer home the delicate nature of their confinement, Coleridge had ordered Cutter's oldest daughter, college sophomore Madeline, to be beaten with a lead pipe live on camera for their viewing pleasure. He then promised that things could and would grow much, much worse for everyone if his orders were not followed explicitly to the letter.

Coleridge smirked and was about to order the execution of Cutter's youngest son when the computer dinged. Instead of ordering another murder, he soaked in the look of defeat that crossed the army general's face. If possible, the man looked even paler.

"Your turn," he said, clapping Nealy on the shoulder.

When Nealy was named acting president, Coleridge's authorization codes had been deactivated. Nealy removed a plastic card known as the "biscuit" from his pocket and cracked off one end to reveal a circuit. He plugged this into a port on the side of the computer and lowered his head to meet the laptop's camera for the retinal scan.

The authorization software processed the data and, in accordance with its two-man rule programming, waited for the secretary of defense to input his authorization code.

Using preset war plans developed during the height of the Cold War, Nealy's aide entered in a string of commands to Milstar, a military communications space satellite in geosynchronous orbit with Earth. From Milstar, the orders were issued to the National Military Command Center and NORAD to launch multiple intercontinental ballistic missiles in a preemptive nuclear strike against Russia.

Moments later, the laptop dinged with incoming messages of orders received and sent back for reverification. Tightening his grip on the man's throat, David pushed Furth forward to re-enter his authorization codes.

One of the things Coleridge found most interesting in America's handling of nuclear arms was its unfathomable simplicity. The entire plan for launching nukes hinged solely on confirming the identities of those in charge and the authenticity of the orders issued. There existed no safeguards to ensure that the commander in chief was acting sanely or that he wasn't behaving under a state of duress. He recalled an incident back in the 1970s when an air force general had been

discharged for even daring to ask how he could know if the orders he received to launch missiles came from a sane president. The entire system was built on rational order and the assurance that the people in charge were responsible actors. It relied solely on trust.

That's the beauty of power, Coleridge thought. *When you have power absolutely, you have trust implicitly. Afterall, who would want to risk pissing off a man who could end billions of lives in a matter of minutes?* The president of the United States could launch the nation's entire arsenal of nukes without anyone second-guessing him, provided the authentications were valid. He didn't have to consult Congress or the Courts. All he had to do was press a few buttons—or make the people who had those buttons push it for him.

Another round of messages passed between the Milstar satellite and the nuclear football. Then a new window popped up. It read: 00:04:00.

00:03:59

00:03:58

00:03:57

The orders had been sent and confirmed, and in less than four minutes, the Earth would burn in a nuclear holocaust. Heated by the ash of nuclear cinders, this world would be ready for Moloch to at last claim it for himself, and sitting at the right hand of all that immense power would be Tyler Coleridge. Blessed with immortality in exchange for his service, Coleridge would live to rule over whatever remnants of America survived as his people were enslaved by Moloch's demonic army.

Coleridge's erection throbbed painfully against his zipper. He wished Evelyn were here with him.

He turned his attention to the monitors broadcasting a secure channel to the various cells of the 88 Blades holding the Joint Chiefs'

families. "Do with them what you will," he said then turned off the monitor. Let the generals and the admiral imagine the fates of their wives, daughters, and sons.

"Kill them," he said to Nealy and David.

The throats of Nealy's military aide and Coleridge's Secretary of Defense were torn out, leaving fist-sized holes from which blood geysered across the shiny, polished table. The two men slumped over, their faces smacking the reflective surface as their lives drained away.

Aghast, General Cutter rushed for the door, the other Joint Chiefs on his heels. Cutter threw open the door then collided with the solid torso of a barrel-chested man who had been standing on the other side. He reeled back, nearly tripping on his own feet as he backed into and was caught by the navy admiral. Cutter was reaching for his sidearm when the first bullet struck him point-blank in the forehead, and he went limp, dead in the admiral's arms. The thick soldier entered the meeting room with a cadre of other uniformed men, all of whom had their weapons drawn and proceeded to rake the room with gunfire.

At the table, Furth's leg twitched. His hand flopped. And then his eyes opened. He smiled, the skin tearing as the thing that now breathed life into that body made itself comfortable inside the delicate shell. The military aide seated next to him began to move too.

"Welcome back, boys," Coleridge said, his eyes never leaving the countdown clock situated at the center of the nuclear football computer.

00:03:27

00:03:26

00:03:25

In a little more than three minutes, Coleridge would cease being the president of the United States.

Instead, he would be a god.

FIFTEEN

THE OVERHEAD LIGHTING FLICKERED IN and out of life, the electrical wiring having been chewed up by gunfire. Glass ground noisily beneath their feet as Hutchinson and Iglesias cautiously stepped out of the freight elevator. The corridor stank of blood, smoke, and cordite.

Hands on both grips of the H&K MP-5 submachine gun, trigger finger resting off the trigger, Hutchinson quickly looked both ways. To the left, the corridor dead ended at a solid wall pockmarked with bullet holes. Nobody was there, save for a single dead soldier whose severed head rested in his lap. To the right, the concrete tunnel stretched on. The golf carts that had served as the primary means of transportation to the heart of the underground complex were tipped over and riddled with holes.

Rushing forward in a half crouch, Hutchinson made his way to one of the overturned carts and ducked behind it. He looked back to the elevator and signaled Iglesias to come forward.

Muffled gunfire echoed down the corridor. Hutchinson pointed

forward then signaled for Iglesias to follow. Although he was reasonably certain there was no way for somebody to come up behind them, Iglesias routinely checked their six as they hustled down the corridor. And although they were both on the same radio channel and had their curlicue earpieces in, he wanted to maintain radio silence lest they give away their presence, especially since the area outside of the elevator had been all but abandoned.

Red lines marred the walls and floor, but aside from the single corpse they'd seen earlier, there were no bodies.

Quietly, they hurried through the two-mile-long stretch of smooth tunnel to the vault-like entrance to the heart of the Deep Underground Command Center itself.

The multistory DUCC was virtually a small city unto itself, manned 24-7 by the US military. Built four thousand feet below ground, it was a secure environment for the president and his staff to escape to in the event of an emergency. The underground bunker included a press briefing room, incinerators to dispose of dead bodies, a self-contained air supply, massive fuel tanks to power its generators, and backup systems that would keep the entire operation running after the loss of power. It was meant to provide shelter in the event of a nuclear attack and preserve not only the government but also life itself in the months and years following such an event. Built to withstand multiple direct hits from massive nuclear missiles, the DUCC could support upward of a thousand souls for more than a year post-attack.

Outfitted with secure satellite communications and hardened against the EMP shock waves generated in a nuclear blast, the DUCC also held several years' worth of food and ammunition stores, as well as medical supplies, a surgical theater and intensive care unit, radiation decontamination showers, and personal protective equipment

to protect against chemicals, radioactive particles and gases, and viral contagion.

In normal times, the DUCC was usually staffed by fifty service-people, but a labyrinth of tunnels connected it to other underground bases and sections of metropolitan DC, allowing the functions of the DUCC to expand even further. Hutchinson had no way of knowing how many people were down there presently or how many of them were safe—or, worse, how many of them were a threat.

The vault entrance was unsealed, its twenty-three-ton blast door hanging open, and he stepped through carefully, gun at the ready.

He felt the air shift and the lizard part of his brain took control. He darted back as a black wand slashed through the air where he'd been standing. His attacker, clad in a dark suit, pressed forward and swung again. Hutchinson stepped into the swing and pinned their arm against his ribs, then he pushed backward on his heel while their weight was off-center, using the force of their momentum against them and pulling them off their feet. He spun and dropped his attacker to the floor, snatching their ASP baton away from them mid-fall.

He saw the flash of long black hair whip in the air as his attacker, a woman, somersaulted and sprang to her feet, reaching for the Glock 9mm holstered at her hip.

Hutchinson breathed a sigh of relief seeing that Colette was fine. Hand on the pistol grip of her sidearm, Colette drew the weapon and aimed. And then her eyes widened in recognition.

"Oh my God," she said, putting her arms around him.

He didn't want to let go, but as Iglesias approached, he forced his body to disengage.

"Nice moves," Iglesias said.

"Colette, this is—"

"Victoria Iglesias," Colette said, bumping her fist against the proffered knuckles Iglesias held out.

"We trained together at the academy."

Hutchinson nodded, pleased they wouldn't have to waste time on introductions, and got down to business. "What's the sitrep?"

"It's fucked," Colette said.

Looking around the room, Hutchinson could only nod.

They were standing in the hub of the DUCC—the nerve center of the entire complex. From here, the president, his staff, and the military could coordinate with other arms of the US government as well as foreign governments around the globe. It also provided direct access to underground installations near the Pentagon; NORAD's Combat Operations Center & Space Defense facility two thousand feet beneath Cheyenne Mountain; the underground Mount Weather Emergency Operation Center in Virginia, where members of Homeland Security and the executive branch would shelter; and the Raven Rock Mountain Complex.

Display screens were shattered, work terminals blasted apart, and the ground was littered with disemboweled bodies and dismembered limbs. The overhead lights flickered like a strobe light, alternating the room between dimly lit and deeply shadowed.

Something heavy crashed to the ground deeper in the complex, its metallic ringing echoing through the cavernous chamber. More gunfire followed, then the screams of a painful death.

The noise of running feet drew closer, and the three Secret Service agents sought cover behind the various work terminals and desks that comprised the open office floor plan. Louder cries drowned out the stomping footfalls, and through all of that was the inhuman wailing and barking of something other, something alien.

Soldiers stepped into the complex, firing at whatever chased

them as they searched for a way to contain the threat and secure the upper hand.

Hutchinson noticed some were firing at hip level, while others had their weapons trained on the ceiling. He couldn't help but think of how Stephen Coleridge had dropped on him from the ceiling of the Oval Office like a spider springing its trap. He swore softly as he focused on his section of the room, trusting Colette and Iglesias to cover their own regions of the op center.

As the lights strobed, he caught a flash of swift movement in the darkened recesses of the ceiling and saw, as illumination returned and disappeared again, a soldier at the back of the line get pulled off his feet. A wet crunch echoed through the room, and the soldier's legs shook, as if he were dancing in midair. Then the body fell and collapsed on the floor like a dropped rag doll. A moment later, the head followed, rolling to a stop against the leg of a nearby workstation. Its dead eyes found Hutchinson, and he quickly looked away, as if he'd just been caught staring.

The dead stormed into the room, their inhuman voices screeching in a language he couldn't understand. While they were clad in military fatigues and the dark business suits of the Secret Service, there was little left of them that was recognizable. Their bodies had mutated in strange and disparate ways, their hands twisted into now-all-too-familiar claws that reminded Hutchinson of the blades of a blender far more than anything human. Their feet, too, were similarly deformed and weaponized; wicked, bony hooks that had once been toes had torn apart boots and shoes alike. Flames burned from between the cracks of their broken desert-like faces, their teeth stretching painfully beyond the confines of their mouths to peel back split lips. Bone jutted sharply from skin and clothing at the elbows and knees, and each body was drawn and extended, giving the sol-

diers and agents rangy, lanky figures that bent and hinged on unnatural joints and segmented limbs. Yellow-and-black eyes scanned
the room, and as one, the creatures howled, an entire cluster of apex
predators starving for prey.

Hutchinson poked his head and submachine gun over the top of
the workstation he knelt behind and opened fire, strafing the group.
The other survivors took his cue and opened fire, as well.

"Aim for their heads," he shouted, noticing then just how malformed the demons' skulls had become. They were elongated and
narrow, save for the mouths, which jutted outward on overly muscled jaws and cavernous maws. Horns grew along the sides of their
heads or from the crown, some small, others longer and tapering to
pointed tips.

A 9mm round from Hutchinson's H&K shattered a grouping
of such horns, and the beast howled in pain as a dark groove carved
a trench along the top of its head. It bounded forward then leaped
onto the ceiling, where it crawled deeper into the op center.

"They're going up!" an unfamiliar voice shouted.

Sparks flew as gunfire chased after the demon above. Nearby,
another voice shouted, "Frag out!"

A few seconds later, an explosion rocked the room. Hutchinson
couldn't hear anything aside from a high-pitched whine in both ears.

Zombies, mutants, demons—whatever the hell they were, the
grenade had helped chop them down a bit. Unfortunately, they were
still moving, dragging their torn-apart bodies forward. With one or
two hands slapping against the floor and shoving them forward, they
reminded Hutchinson, perversely, of how sea lions used their flippers
to walk. Those that could scrambled up the walls and to the ceilings,
shouting and screeching guttural commands.

Bullets tore fresh holes into the deformed creatures, but few head-

shots were made. They moved so fast, it was hard to pin them down, or even get an accurate count of how many there were. Hutchinson put the opposing force at twenty men, more than double the defending team of military and Secret Service.

"Watch out!" he shouted toward one servicewoman, who looked up and swung her weapon into place simultaneously.

She fired a three-round burst into the torso of the descending beast, whose falling weight crushed her to the floor. Her rifle skittered across the slate tiles, out of reach. She tried to shove the monster away with one hand even as she freed her backup sidearm, a Beretta M9. Large teeth snapped at her face, and she brought her forearm up into the thing's throat, straining to push that alien face away. Drool leaked from its bloody lips, and strings of thick, pink drool splashed against her cheek.

She brought the M9 up and jammed the muzzle against the side of the monstrosity's head and pulled the trigger. The opposite side of the creature's head exploded outward, and she shoved the corpse away, putting another round through the front of its head, right between the eyes. Then, she took a knee and spun back toward the front of the room, seeking out a new target.

Another soldier farther ahead was not so lucky. Hutchinson couldn't get a clear shot around the sea of desks to save him, but he could hear the snapping of oversized teeth far too well and the screams that followed. Then a thick gout of red exploded into the air, chased by a handful of entrails. It was like watching a much-gorier rendition of the Yellowstone geyser venting columns of water into the air.

The survivors had arrayed themselves around the room in a half circle, cautious not to end up in another's line of fire. The monsters enjoyed a much larger playfield, though, able to easily take the high

ground by traveling across the ceiling to drop down on the people below. The battle was frustrating, and as it went on, Hutchinson could feel morale plummeting as soldiers were picked off with increasing frequency. He and the others had managed to kill the mutated soldiers, but they were still outnumbered two to one. Those weren't good odds, and they were getting worse.

He fired at a flash of movement above, but his shot went wide. From above, the creature lunged down toward him, and Hutchinson had to roll out of the way before the thing fell on top of him. He kicked out a foot, snapping the bony protuberance off the thing's knee, earning a high-pitched squeal. On his back, he brought up his weapon and fired a three-round burst into the center of the monster's face. A grapefruit-sized hole exploded out the back of the creature's head, and the mauled corpse dropped, completely lifeless.

Iglesias and Colette were both backed against a corner on opposite sides of the room, but they engaged the enemy with ruthless proficiency. A litter of dead bodies lay at their feet as the heads of their targets were blasted apart.

He trusted them and their training to get them through the next few minutes. They were strong and capable women. He knelt behind the desk once again and took up fire against the oncoming horde, alternating between those crawling by hand across the floor and those stabbing their way across the ceiling.

Hutchinson shot off the knife-like fingers of an approaching beast then centered on its head. Just as he fired, the creature lifted its head toward the sky and let out a blood-curdling howl that was cut short as Hutchinson's rounds tore through its neck. The thing's head popped loose and rolled between its outstretched arms, face frozen mid-screech.

A shotgun boomed nearby, and Hutchinson glanced that way in

time to see another creature's head dissolve in a spray of bloody pulp. Emboldened, the shooter stepped forward toward another one of the crawlers and put his boot down in the middle of the thing's back. He lowered the shotgun so that the muzzle was resting against the back of its skull and blew its head off. Gore showered across him.

Hutchinson saw another crawler scrambling across the wall beside him, using the shadows for cover. "Ten o'clock," he yelled, drawing on the horror with his Glock.

The shotgunner dove out of the way, giving Hutchinson the opening he needed.

The room stank of foul musk, and the air ventilation system was working overtime to suck the smoke up and out of the room. The odor hung strong, thick and cloying.

For a moment, the room was very quiet, and nobody moved. Then somebody whooped loudly. A victory cheer.

Hutchinson looked around the room at all the corpses that were strewn about. Somehow, they'd won. All the monsters were down, many of them little more than tattered torsos after all of the gunfire.

He breathed deeply, the adrenaline of combat already rushing out of his system and leaving him exhausted.

"We have to find Coleridge," he said.

"Who do you think did all this?" said a young man dressed in air force blues.

"You know where he is?"

"EO," the airman said. The Executive Office. "Last I saw anyway."

"You know where it is?" asked an older, gruffer man in army fatigues. He had two silver bars on his uniform blouse.

"I've been here before," Hutchinson said, recalling the three days he'd spent in the DUCC while Coleridge hid from BLM protestors

marching outside a completely darkened White House. Although Coleridge often refused to take part, the Secret Service routinely conducted practice drills to test the efficacy of their emergency-escape plans in a variety of scenarios. One of those drills had tested their response time to evacuate the president into the DUCC, taking him from either the Oval Office or the Residence and to the West Wing or the basement freight elevator. Hutchinson was confident he knew this facility better than Coleridge.

"Captain, what's it like down there? Any idea?" Hutchinson turned toward the corridor leading out of the op center and to the rooms beyond. Farther down that shaft were offices for military command, and at the opposite end were stairs and elevators for accessing the floors below.

Directly beneath them was the president's state room and en suite, a rather plush recreation of the White House Residence—that would be guarded at all times. That floor also served as the executive command level, with a large executive office that could seat the president, his staff, advisors, and cabinet, along with additional military personnel and officials. It was essentially a recreation of the five-thousand-square-foot White House Situation Room and its attendant offices, and like the Sit Room, it was staffed by watch teams composed of National Security Council personnel. What concerned Hutchinson was the unknown number of potential threats that awaited him down there. It was unlikely the EO Sit Room had been fully staffed with the thirty duty officers who comprised the five watch teams that rotated in and out of service to monitor global events 24-7.

The army captain spoke again. "Acting President Nealy and the cabinet were situated down there."

"We had other agents stationed with them as well," Colette said. "Nealy's dead, Mike. He's one of them now."

Hutchinson nodded. He supposed that explained why Colette was up here rather than with Nealy. The fact that she had been alone chilled him. "The rest of your detail?"

She shook her head.

"Damn it," he said softly. He could hear the tiredness in his own voice, and his arms and legs felt heavy with overuse. He inspected his weapons, slid in fresh ammo mags, and resecured his Glock at his hip. "Captain, you and these men and women keep this room secure. I want the hatch sealed. Nothing gets in or out of this facility. Do not let anybody into this control room. See what you can do about getting our communications back online. Iglesias and Bridges, you're with me."

***

Quietly moving down the stairs, Hutchinson followed the hand-guard LED light attached to the H&K. As with the operations center above, many of the lights on the Executive Level had been destroyed, and those that remained flickered or hung loose from their damaged ceiling mounts.

As he stepped off the lowest riser and onto level ground, his shoes squished against something solid and slippery. Organs and chunks of meat were strewn across the length of the corridor, and chaotic splatter marks painted the white walls red. A noxious fecal stench hung in the air, and dense clouds of flies shifted in the gun's light. As he led Iglesias and Bridges down the hall, he saw clods of shit on the floor, as if somebody had marked their territory. He wondered if Coleridge had been the one to defecate there and realized he really couldn't put it past the man, whether human or demon. It was difficult to say whether the puddles up and down the length of the shaft were water

or urine. The blood, however, was much easier to identify.

The Executive Level had a larger floor plan than the upper level with its presidential suite, several master bedrooms for the family, and living and dining rooms, as well as a private library. Positioned before the residence, though, was the work area, which Hutchinson and his two companions reached first.

One by one, they worked their way through the various offices arranged there as swiftly and silently as possible. Hutchinson could feel the tension boiling over as he wondered what was behind each door, keenly aware that an attack could come at any moment. Although they found nothing, none of them could afford to become complacent or assume their safety was assured.

"We're clear here," Iglesias said, exiting the NSA's work space.

"VP's office is clear," Colette said. Her dark skin was shiny with sweat.

Even though the temperature in the DUCC was regulated and kept a constant and comfortable seventy-two degrees, nerves and strain had gotten to each of them. Hutchinson's shirt was soaked through, and dark rings circled his underarms. His clothes were all but glued to his body, and he wiped at his forehead with the back of one arm.

Farther down the corridor was a much larger suite of offices for the commander in chief and the attendant offices that comprised the Situation Room, the NSC Watch Center, and a video conferencing room. The offices were darkened, but as the Secret Service agents entered and fanned out across the room, the motion-activated lights sprang to life and covered the room in a soft white glow.

"Contact!" Iglesias shouted and immediately opened fire with her assault rifle.

The head of one of Coleridge's cabinet members dissolved in a

pulpy red mist. The rest of the cabinet bounded across the Watch Center desks, scurrying on hands and feet like rabid dogs hunting fresh meat. Others launched onto the walls and ceiling.

Lights exploded in a shower of sparks as Hutchinson sprayed the ceiling with bullets, casting the room back into darkness. The eight former cabinet members were insanely fast, but Hutchinson still managed to eliminate two of them. Trying to find cover against the abominations was all but pointless. As soon as his light fell on the sallow snarling face of the secretary of education, he blew out the back of her head. As her body fell, he swiveled to the next target, the deformed EPA administrator, and killed him too.

Colette and Iglesias methodically cut down as many as they could, covering one another as they exchanged spent mags for fresh ones.

Before Colette could get a fresh magazine in her Glock, Bob Highter, the US trade rep, leaped across a Watch Center desk. The telephone and darkened dual-display computer monitors went flying as he crashed into them and sprang off his hands, aiming straight for Colette. Iglesias fired, but Highter was too quick and absorbed the impacts with his disemboweled torso. He bowled into Colette. Her gun and spare mag skittered across the floor in opposite directions as she hit the floor. The air audibly rushed out of her lungs, but she was fast too.

Her reflexes and training took over immediately. She brought a knee up between them and, as she kicked him off, grabbed the spare gun holstered at her ankle. Colette twisted on one knee, bringing the weapon around in a smooth, fluid movement, and shot Highter point-blank in the head. His skull thudded against the floor.

Iglesias and Hutchinson kept up their assault while Colette pressed herself up against the desk and began firing over the top.

They managed to eliminate the last two threats and bought themselves some time to breathe and reload once again.

Hutchinson was thankful the entire twenty-three-member cabinet hadn't been down here. They'd gotten lucky. Unfortunately, it raised the question of where the others were. Were they alive, or had they been transformed by whatever dark forces Coleridge had somehow summoned?

As if in answer to his silent questions, he caught a flicker of movement at the opposite end of the room. A soft glow emanated from beyond the door of the Executive Office. Shadows flickered and moved inside.

He pointed at his eyes then motioned toward the far end of the Watch Center. Colette and Iglesias both nodded, waiting for his next order. Using tactical hand signals, he directed them to stay low and move forward.

In the dark, their gun lights extinguished, they crept forward quietly, concealing themselves behind and alongside the desks arranged between them and the large Executive Office. The EO was a spacious suite divided into two halves, making it a rough amalgamation of the White House's Oval Office and Briefing Room. Instead of the more comfortable and less formal seating arrangement of sofas and chairs in the Oval Office, there was a long, polished oak table situated on a raised platform that could comfortably seat fourteen. Additional chairs were spaced out around the platform. Despite the luster of wood and leather and the cutting-edge technology, there was no mistaking the Briefing Room for what it really was—a war room.

Hutchinson ordered his shooters to stop, and they took cover behind the desks. He moved in closer and used the wall for cover, looking around the entry. Coleridge and Nealy were standing in

profile to his spot beside the entryway, and Hutchinson saw the full extent of the president's transformation. In addition to the wickedly sharp assembly of long segmented, bony fingers, the rest of the man's body had changed as well. Coleridge's precious hair had sloughed away, and the flaccid flesh of his face hung around the skull, giving him the appearance of melting wax. Two enormous and thick horns stood from his skull and curled out around the sides of his head, like a bighorn ram's.

Nealy was on his knees in front of Coleridge, and the president was masturbating over the open mouth of what had once been the most prim and devoutly Catholic man inside the Beltway. Coleridge's eyes were squeezed shut, and he was muttering a name over and over.

"Evelyn," he moaned, "Oh, Evelyn, yes, just like that, sweetie, oh yes. Don't stop, Evelyn. Don't you stop!"

Hutchinson could see much too clearly as Coleridge stroked the thin rod of his mushroom-headed cock. The president grabbed Nealy's head and pulled him forward, stuffing his erection into the VP's waiting mouth. As he face-fucked the vice president, his fingers pulled Nealy's hair, tearing away chunks of the man's scalp in long, bloody strips to reveal sharply studded bone held together by flame.

Coleridge's thrusting grew more intense, his starkly pale, sagging buttocks heaving with each gyration. He cried his daughter's name as he came, exploding into the ruined, half-skinned face of his second-in-command. Nealy sat back on his heels and, with the sleeve of his suit coat, wiped away the jizz dribbling from his lips and down his chin.

As Coleridge pulled up his pants, Hutchinson knew he wouldn't have a better chance than this. He centered his gun sights on the side of Coleridge's head, took a steadying breath, and fired.

The 9mm bullet blasted into the side of the thick horn.

Coleridge's head snapped to the side, and he stumbled briefly but recovered fast. He shook his head, annoyed. Nealy shot to his feet.

Another round of gunfire exploded from behind Hutchinson—from Colette or Iglesias, he didn't know—and blasted off the top of Nealy's head. The light from his eyes and between the sutures of his skull extinguished, and his body dropped to the floor.

Coleridge howled, loud and bear-like, as he turned toward the agents. The noise of it hurt Hutchinson's ears, and he felt a wet trickle down one side of his head.

Coleridge's fingers grabbed hold of the loose skin over his face and pulled. A sheet of flesh tore away from bone, gooey strings of fat and muscle pulling taut and snapping.

The president's skull was a far cry from that of a human. It looked far more animalistic, but even then, there were differences. As he opened his mouth to scream, Hutchinson noted extra rows of shark-like teeth, and his jaws pushed out on either side to make room for the extra dentata. Flames danced within the hollows of his bones, burning brightly from within his sinus cavity and behind his eyes.

As Coleridge bellowed, his sloppy gore-streaked suit jacket and shirt began to tear. A massive pair of leathery wings sprouted from the president's back and fanned out on either side of him.

Hutchinson fired again, once, twice, then a third time, but the bullets buried themselves uselessly in armor-like plates of bone. Coleridge's skull was impossibly thick.

The president screamed again, and Hutchinson realized it was a language of sorts. He couldn't understand the words, but he didn't have to.

David Coleridge stood from the chair he was sitting in and stepped up onto the conference table. The younger man was wild-

ly disfigured, caught somewhere between human and demonic animal, but as he moved, his limbs pulled tightly at the confines of his clothes, threatening to rend the garments from his body.

Hutchinson pushed into the room, unthinking. He fired with each step he took, but his weapon seemed to only annoy Coleridge. The president slammed into him, knocking him off his feet.

Coleridge grabbed him by his throat, his sharp talons drawing painful lines along either side of Hutchinson's neck, and lifted him off his feet.

Wings battered at Hutchinson's body, then he was slammed back into the ground. All of the air left his body, and he blinked groggily. His head rebounded off the floor, and his entire body lit up with pain. He gasped and wheezed as his lungs struggled to take in air. Coleridge's hand closed over his face, suffocating him, and he felt razorblades split his scalp open, blood sheeting down his back.

Through a gap between a pair of Coleridge's fingers, he saw David leap off the table and onto the president's back. David's savage hooked nails scraped across the bone of Coleridge's skull.

The older, larger demon was shocked at the sudden attack, and he released Hutchinson's head. In the process, his claws raked across the agent's face, tearing his skin into ribbons. Coleridge shouted something inhuman and angry while his son scratched at his eyes.

***

"This world is mine," David shouted. "All of this is *mine!*"

Coleridge wobbled, trying to maintain his balance, as David pressed his feet against his father's back and looped his hands through the curls of Coleridge's horns. The president's wings whipped through the air, angling back in an effort to dislodge his son, but it

was useless. David straightened his legs and flexed his arms, pulling on the horns and snapped Coleridge's head back with a shockingly loud crack.

Coleridge loosed an inhuman shriek of pain, his talons scrabbling for his son, but he couldn't reach far enough back to interrupt David's plans. His long, jagged nails scraped uselessly against David's powerful frame. Coleridge tottered backward again as David viciously yanked on his bony horns, then he was falling.

David rode his father to the ground, getting out from under the man in time to prevent being crushed beneath him. Coleridge's claws encircled David's muscled wrists as David planted a foot in the center of his father's chest. With a roar, David sharply twisted the horns—and the head they were attached to. Coleridge's neck snapped loudly, and his cries were instantly silenced.

David twisted farther, and the loud cracking of bones popping and tendons tearing filled the room. The baggy skin around Coleridge's neck drew tight then tore with a papery rasp. A swarm of roaches filed out from beneath the ripping flesh, scattering in the light of the room. David pulled harder, his face pinching in strain, and tore the man's burning head free, ripping loose a part of the president's spinal column with it. Flies buzzed out of the stump of the president's bloodless neck. Maggots squirmed all along the tail of dangling vertebrae, while other insects darted around the roughly torn flaps of skin dangling from Coleridge's head, seeking new hidey-holes. David turned, trophy in hand, a leering smile on his face.

A whisper of shifting air was the only warning he had, and he met the powerful swing of a collapsible metal baton head-on. His cheekbone collapsed beneath the impact and rattled loose a pair of razor-sharp teeth. He bit off the side of his tongue as he stumbled backward, his feet twisting painfully over the form of his dead father.

The ASP baton hammered down on him again, shattering his nose and tearing loose the soft flesh of his upper lip.

"You won't ever win," he said, looking up at the black woman as she swung again.

A lighter, brown-skinned woman raised her thick boot over his face and smashed her heel through his mouth, shattering his teeth and leaving him with a mouthful of jagged shrapnel.

David's laughter turned into wet gurgling as he tried to stand, but the women refused to grant him any quarter as they swung and stomped on him. Searing, otherworldly pain rang through his head, followed by a head-rattling crack.

The last thing he saw was the sole of a boot smashing toward him, and then the world went dark.

***

Colette was breathing hard, her arms and shoulders aching from all the swinging. She nodded to Iglesias, letting her know their work was done.

Iglesias nodded back then stepped away, panting hard as she wiped her hands on the thighs of her pants.

At their feet, David Coleridge's head was a lumpy pudding, large plates of shattered skull floating like islands in an ocean of blood. Brain matter was ground into the carpet, and one unseeing eye dangled loosely down the side of his cratered head.

Iglesias was covered in splatter and greasy chunks of brain, her black boots shiny with a thick coat of red.

Both women slumped against the wall, and Colette looked toward Hutchinson's still form.

"Oh my God," she said, scrambling across the carpet on hands

and knees to be at his side. Her heart was racing with fear. "No, no, no, no, no."

In the time it took to cross those few feet to reach him, a thousand awful thoughts swirled through her head simultaneously, each of them terminating at one dark conclusion.

Hutchinson's head was ringed in blood, and it looked like somebody had tried to peel open his face. She knew head wounds bled aggressively, but even this seemed excessive, and she knew then that he was dead. Plasma was pouring from his scalp and face and from shallower gouges on both sides of his neck. If the carotid had been nicked then…

"Stay with me, Hutch, baby. Stay with me," she said, repeating the words over and over like a mantra. She knew it wasn't wise to move him without knowing the extent of his injuries. She'd seen him get slammed into the ground, and a moment's hesitation swept through her as her brain reminded her of potential spinal damage.

She made a rapid-fire decision and shifted him so that his head was in her lap. If he was dead, or if he was going to die, then she at least wanted him to have this brief moment of comfort.

Blood flowed over her fingers as she searched for a pulse. He was still alive, but the thrum of his heartbeat was slow and thready. His eyes fluttered open, only for half a breath, but in that instant, he saw her. He smiled.

He was alive. *Still alive, oh yes, God, oh sweet lord, still alive.*

It was the world that was dead.

***

"Oh shit," Iglesias said, interrupting Colette's reverie. Colette was maneuvering Hutchinson's head into her lap, but it wasn't the dam-

age to Hutchinson that earned her invective.

Rather, it was the laptop sitting in the center of the massive oak table. The laptop had only a single image on its display—a timer. It showed only zeroes.

She turned her attention to the various television monitors mounted on the wall around the table. Some showed breaking news alerts from the nation's biggest cable news channels, while others showed overhead satellite imagery. Both amounted to the same, and her hand went to her quivering lips.

Iglesias fell to her knees, her face buried in both hands. Colette shifted and pulled the woman to her, Iglesias's weight falling against her. She took it and held on to the woman, her jaw clenched tightly as she stared hard at the satellite feeds. Iglesias's tears were hot against her neck.

On the various split-screen images on the display monitors, a bright light flashed across major US cities, its hot whiteness spreading fast, growing brighter until it washed out all the details on each screen, then darkened. One by one, each feed went deathly black.

The DUCC was too far below the earth to feel the shaking, rumbling detonations of the retaliatory nuclear strikes pulverizing the streets and buildings of Washington, DC, above them.

Colette didn't know what else to do, so she simply held on to the two bodies on either side of her. Neither woman spoke. What was there to say, after all? She and Iglesias hardly knew each other, but in that moment of trauma, they knew all they needed to. If anything, they knew too much.

From elsewhere within in the complex, the sounds of gunfire rattled through the air.

SIXTEEN

HUTCHINSON'S FACE WAS BRUISED AND swollen. The skin around the stitches holding his face together was red and puffy. An army medic had done her best to put him back together, but he looked like a jigsaw puzzle of a railroad map. Even with the courses of antibiotics and painkillers he was on, he was in constant agony.

Over the few hours it had taken to stitch him up, the military had been able to root out the rest of the demons and eliminate what remained of Coleridge's malformed cabinet. They'd suffered heavy losses in the process but still managed to carry the day, for whatever that was worth. They'd worked into the early morning hours of the next day to secure the DUCC and reestablish the operations center's communications terminals. With the amount of damage the op center had suffered, the job was neither easy nor quick, and the technicians had to salvage, rewire, and jury-rig new terminals from parts of the old.

Hutchinson was in the bathroom, unraveling the bloody gauze from around his head, when he heard an outbreak of applause. His

wounds were seeping, and he debated putting on fresh bandages, but he'd felt too trapped beneath the layers of fabric. Colette had encouraged him to rest, but he needed to see what was happening. He dropped the stained gauze into the sink and went to investigate.

Colette had stayed with him while the medic did her work, and she knew how bad he looked. As for the rest of the men and women in the op center… when they caught sight of him, their mouths fell open, and they hurried to cast their eyes elsewhere. Only a few of them had ever seen worse.

"Jesus, boss," Iglesias said, tilting her head to get a better look at his scalp and the back of his head. She examined him like he was a fresh specimen under a microscope, and he wondered about her morbid curiosity. "You look like Frankenstein," she said, actually sounding impressed.

"What's happening?" he asked. One of Coleridge's claws had slit his cheek almost all the way through, and the stitches made it difficult to move his mouth. He spoke softly and carefully, like he was performing a ventriloquist act using his own body as the wooden dummy.

"We've managed to reach Mount Weather," an army captain said. "They're getting Speaker Sherman to a terminal now."

More applause broke out, but it felt muted. It died quickly as House Speaker Madeline Sherman settled into a chair and stared into a computer monitor. Her face was pale, but her eyes still held an enormous strength. She met Hutchinson's ribboned face with a steely gaze.

"What's your status?" she asked, cutting through any formalities. "Is the president—" She stumbled, unsure what to say next or how to ask the proper questions.

"Madame Speaker," Hutchinson said, stepping forward. Every-

one's eyes were on him now. "President Coleridge is dead, as is Vice President Nealy, and the president's cabinet."

Her face managed to turn even whiter as the implications sank in. She was now acting president of the United States of America.

"Is President-Elect Barnett with you?" he asked, aware that the man had been in his Virginia home with his family. It would make sense for the Secret Service team assigned to protect him to evac him to Mount Weather. The question was whether or not they would have made it there in time.

"He is," Sherman confirmed.

Hutchinson breathed a sigh of relief. It hurt.

In the hours that followed, he was able to piece together a rough timeline. When the attacks on the capitol began and the 88 Blades led an assault on the White House, Capitol police had begun the evacuation of the members of Congress and were able to secure House and Senate leadership. Although the 117th United States Congress was not officially in session, many of the elected representatives had been in DC to be sworn in and had been safely evacuated.

Once it was confirmed Coleridge had initiated the attack by the 88 Blades upon the White House via his Twitter account, the Secret Service had immediately taken Barnett, his wife, his two adult children, their spouses, and one bull mastiff to a secure location, the underground Mount Weather installation. Barnett and his family were safe inside well before Coleridge had initiated a nuclear strike and the world responded.

Four minutes had passed between Coleridge's launch of the nation's nuclear arsenal and the destruction of Moscow. Twelve minutes after that, the first of Russia's retaliatory strikes hit California, and additional missiles were in the air to New York, Washington, DC, and nations allied to the US, like England and France. Within a half

hour of Coleridge's commands, almost the entire world was burning as nations fell in rounds of mutually assured destruction. Entire countries had toppled like dominoes—all because of one man's ego and narcissism. Coleridge's lust for power, his sense of entitlement and unwillingness to let go of the reins of the presidency had killed much of the world in a single, vastly sweeping "fuck you" to everyone.

Hutchinson sat back in his chair, his entire head on fire with pain. He rubbed at his eyes, but even that stung as his fingers tugged on delicately tender flesh. At least Coleridge, that psychopath, was dead. It was up to Marcus Barnett to salvage whatever he could of this country in the months and years ahead and, once the fallout settled, work on rebuilding.

The fallout. Hutchinson couldn't help but laugh grimly. There was certain to be plenty of that, and in more ways than one. The fallout of Coleridge's entire presidency. The fallout from nuclear war.

If the generals were to be believed, the nuclear fallout would decay rather quickly. Nobody seemed to agree on how long it would take to begin reconstruction efforts, and the idea that American cities would be able to recover as quickly as Hiroshima and Nagasaki had following World War II sounded foolishly optimistic. Modern nuclear payloads were much larger than those of the past, and one of the largest in America's arsenal was the B83 warhead, which was sixty times more powerful than the twenty-kiloton Fat Man bomb that had been dropped on Nagasaki seventy-five years earlier.

Russia's nuclear arsenal had been the largest in the world, and early intelligence reports showed that America and its closest allies had taken the brunt of their sixteen hundred actively deployed missiles. One of their torpedoes, a one-hundred-megaton nuke, was designed to create a massive radioactive tsunami that would wash across

its target's shores. Based on satellite reconnaissance, officials believed such a weapon had indeed been launched against the US's western seaboard and that it had generated massively irradiated waves more than sixteen hundred feet tall.

Hutchinson shuddered at the thought of all those people dying so miserably. It would be a long time before this country would ever be united again. And that was, perhaps, the worst fallout of all. Coleridge had spent four years dividing and tearing apart this nation and its people, turning men into monsters, well before his last desperate attack to retain power.

Like a cult leader, he had twisted so many hearts and minds toward evil purposes and showed the world how much hate he and his supporters held. That fallout was the most dangerous kind, and it would last for generations and generations. Coleridge had even managed to destroy the sanctity of death. Whatever door he had opened to allow demons to trespass into this world might never be closed.

Hutchinson stood to stretch his back and immediately felt woozy. He put a hand out to stop himself from falling.

"You okay?" Colette asked, putting an arm around him.

"Stood up too fast," he said. "I gotta go to the bathroom."

She took his hand in hers and walked with him. The concern on her face was plain, and he tried to offer her a reassuring smile, until he imagined how ghastly that must have looked.

He found the men's room and flicked on a light. His face burned, and he had a hard time looking at the damage of his weeping wounds. Blood trickled down his neck, past his collar. He dabbed gently at the cuts with a paper towel.

Maybe it's time I go lie down, he thought, feeling half dead on his feet.

Colette came with him and sat by his side. They didn't talk about

what little was left of the world, what it might be like up above, or how many survivors there might be. They didn't talk at all, and the silence was its own kind of comfort.

Holding on to her hand, Hutchinson closed his eyes slowly. He shivered, suddenly freezing, and she covered him in a blanket, snuggling up against him to give him additional warmth. Within minutes, he was asleep.

***

By the next morning, Hutchinson was looking worse, and Colette was growing more concerned about him. He couldn't stop shaking, and when the medic took his temperature, he was at 102.5 degrees Fahrenheit. In addition to his aching face, he complained of abdominal pains and was looking paler than the night before. He was also having trouble breathing, and the medic was concerned about his increased heart rate.

Colette had seen this play out before in her grandfather a number of years before. Grandpa was chronically ill, and following the removal of a tumor, the incision site had become infected. A short time later, he'd died of septic shock.

Hutchinson was loaded onto a medical gurney and rushed to the DUCC's treatment facility. Unfortunately, given the rushed nature of the evacuation and the chaos that had left so many in the White House dead, there were no full-time medical staff. The sole army medic was the best they had, but Hutchinson needed doctors. He needed blood tests and nurses and God only knew what else.

Colette couldn't help but wonder if whatever was killing him was more than just a simple infection. With all of the gore that had been on Coleridge's bloody claws, it was a safe bet that his dirty

hands would have left behind contaminates, and it was certainly possible that Hutchinson's wounds hadn't been cleaned thoroughly enough. But was that all this was? A simple transfer between filthy fingers and fresh wounds? Or had Coleridge's touch been venomous, like a snake's bite? Had he injected something into Hutchinson that was now killing him? It would be fitting, she supposed. Everything Coleridge had touched, he'd destroyed, either with deliberate purpose or reckless malevolence. She'd always thought the man's touch was poisonous, and now she couldn't help but wonder if it had become literally so in his last reaching grasps to maintain power.

She sighed in frustration, anger, and more than a little bit of hopeless helplessness. There was no way of saying how much, or how deeply, Coleridge was responsible for what was afflicting Hutchinson now. All she knew was that he was in serious trouble, and he needed more help than they had to give.

In the medical bay, Hutchinson was started on an intravenous antibiotic in an attempt to kill the infection, along with additional painkillers. The medic assured Colette she would do everything she could for him, but the words felt half-hearted.

Left in a weakened state, he floated in and out of consciousness, but Colette stayed by his side. Each time his eyes landed on her, there was a spark of recognition and a pained smile. As his temperature dropped, the medic began to grow more hopeful that the antibiotics were working.

Until his temperature dropped too low, dipping below ninety-six degrees Fahrenheit. His breathing grew more rapid and erratic, and when she gave him her hand again, he squeezed it hard.

"I need to see Robbie," he said. Her mouth opened in an O of surprise, and his grip on her hand tightened, hurting her fingers. "Goddamnit, Alicia, let me see him!"

She ripped her hand loose and pushed herself away from him. It was the infection, she knew, that was causing his confusion.

He hadn't spoken of Robbie until that moment, and she wondered whether he realized what had happened or if a part of him was foolishly holding out hope. She knew it was impossible for the boy or his mother to still be alive, but was Hutchinson cognizant of that? Had he forgotten, or was he so broken that he couldn't, or wouldn't, admit it?

She sat back down and met his eyes. "Mike, do you know who I am?"

"I," he said, stammering over his next few words. His voice was weak and shaky, and it took a moment for his eyes to clear in recognition. "I'm sorry. I... lost it there for a minute, I guess."

He closed his eyes again and slept. If he thought Robbie was still alive, perhaps there was no harm in letting him have that belief, at least for a little while. He needed strength to get him through this, and if thoughts of his son, still up there, still breathing, and still alive, helped him, then she couldn't take that away from him.

For the rest of that day, she stayed by his side. She tried to keep her mind occupied with a book she had found in the DUCC's library, but the words were impossible to focus on. She set it aside and watched her lover sleep, watching his vitals digitally etched across the small monitor he was wired to.

Colette had begun to doze when the alarm went off, and the medic rushed in with a crash cart. The machine droned on, and she saw that Hutchinson's heart had flatlined.

The medic pressed a pair of paddles to his chest and shouted, "Clear!" to nobody. An electric current jolted through Hutchinson's body and lifted his back off the bed. Lifeless, his body resettled.

The army medic increased the current and shocked him again.

Numb, Colette sank back into the chair and told the medic to leave. Both of them had seen the reports and heard the briefings that had come down from the upper levels of command. Some called it Coleridge's Legacy in spiteful, bitter tones. The failed president had changed everything—*ruined everything*—and she wondered if life would ever be the same.

Her Glock felt impossibly heavy in her hand, and she let it rest on her thigh, her finger outside the trigger guard.

A moment later, Hutchinson's jigsaw puzzle of a face turned toward her, and his lips twitched. He smiled wider, popping loose several stitches, and she saw, deep inside those wounds, a fiery glow.

He opened his eyes, and they were yellow.

AFTERWORD

Obviously, much of this book was inspired by and written in response to the current state of America circa 2020, but its roots run a little bit deeper than just these past few months. Although I wrote the bulk of this book in the weeks leading up to the 2020 US presidential election and in the insane, tumultuous days that followed, *Friday Night Massacre* had been taking shape in my mind almost daily since the results of the 2016 election hit us and left me gobsmacked. Although he had (rightly) lost the popular vote in 2016, thanks to the rules of our electoral college, the nation had nonetheless elected an authoritarian demagogue in Donald Trump.

Some academics well versed in world history and autocratic regimes suggested we keep a journal of how the world changed around us, because rulers like Trump are so adept at altering reality, along with our perceptions and memories of what had come before, that we might not even notice all we had lost and all that had been taken away from us. I didn't keep a journal, but this book itself was sustained by all of the madness that unraveled in the wake of Trump's

ascendancy and the rise of the MAGA cult, from his campaign trail calls for the jailing and assassination of political rivals to his appearing on live TV and asking a foreign country to hack us.

The overriding question of the four years that followed, then, was not only whether or not we would ever be able to rid ourselves of Trump but what insane shit he was going to do next now that he'd been handed the codes to our nation's nuclear arsenal. Over the course of his, for lack of a better term, "presidency," Trump made it plain, often and regularly, that he was a fascist, a racist, a sexist, a misogynist, and, most of all, a narcissistic, power-hungry, degenerate lunatic with a decades-long obsession with the nuclear might of the United States. He would readily go on, again repeatedly, to prove himself to be a human monster—the type of real-life monster that, in fact, makes perfect fodder for fictional horrors.

For me, much of *Friday Night Massacre* was an exercise in alleviating my own years-long anxiety over the 2020 election and 2020 as a whole, a way to sort of hope for the best while also preparing for the worst. Let's not forget that Trump kicked 2020 off with his attempts to start World War III via his fucking Twitter account! Writing this book was also an act of catharsis. Flat out, I was scared—*terrified*, really—that Donald Trump would eke out another victory.

That didn't happen, regardless of how many tweets he sent out stoking fires, claiming states and victories, and refusing to concede his loss in the days and weeks after the election.

As the news began to break that human morality, after four long years of being beaten and pissed on, had won out against the Trump regime, I wondered if there was a place in the horror genre for this book after all. Perhaps *Friday Night Massacre* was too little, too late.

But then the full scope of the number of ballots cast in Trump's favor began to reveal itself, and the implications of those votes

showed me that I was right to still be concerned. At final count, whether they're willing to admit it to themselves or not, seventy-four million Americans voted in favor of fascism and authoritarianism. Seventy-four million Americans wanted to empower Trump to further erode our freedoms to vote, our freedom of speech, and our free press. They wanted to continue having Mexican children ripped away from their parents and locked in cages. They wanted to keep the COVID-19 pandemic going for at least another four years and deprive an ever-increasing number of us of our right to simply *live*. They wanted to keep seeing journalists harassed and assaulted. They wanted to keep seeing Trump break all the laws and all of the norms of decency that he possibly could. They wanted to keep this madman's tiny fingers on the nuclear button in the hopes that he could, finally, tweet his way into Biblical Armageddon. Hell, as mobs of self-destructive red-hatted cult members stormed election centers and demanded that some states stop the vote while others keep counting, they were literally *praying* for it!

Even now, at the time of this writing, a week after the election, a headline in *The Atlantic* reads, "Just How Badly Does Trump Want Revenge?" Meanwhile, *Washington Post* reporter Toluse Olorunnipa revealed on CNN that Trump was now plotting "a four-year campaign of vengeance." And, despite not having conceded the results of the 2020 election, Trump is already threatening to make another run for the presidency in 2024, but with any luck, he'll be in prison by then. President-elect Biden, meanwhile, is hoping to unite the country, stating in a November seventh address to the nation, "Let this grim era of demonization in America begin to end here and now."

It's a wonderful sentiment, but let's not lose sight of who has to do the hard work here. The onus of reunification lies with those who voted against every single basic tenet of our American democracy.

They need to do the work and show receipts. *They* need to prove they are working on making amends and becoming better human beings who will stand with this country, and the majority of Americans who demand progress, rather than against it. My cynical side says it'll be a hard sell for those seventy-four million racism-loving Americans who can't even begin to fathom basic human decency, let alone supposedly making this country great again.

So, maybe this book wasn't too little, too late after all. I hope it helps serve as a reminder of just how chaotic and insane these last four years have been and will maybe help serve as a warning of what might come if we once more flirt with the deliberate destruction of our republic. Or perhaps it will just be a fun time capsule of an insane period of chaos. Either way, let's not ever do this again, OK, America?

While this book has been percolating in the dark for four long years, bringing it to life was no small feat. In addition to subjecting myself to the daily horrors of the Trump administration as reported by CNN, *The New York Times*, *Washington Post*, and NPR, I read the work of master scholar on authoritarianism, journalist, and co-host of the *Gaslit Nation* podcast, Sarah Kendzior. Kendzior's book *Hiding in Plain Sight: The Invention of Donald Trump and the Erosion of America* is an invaluable source of longform political journalism. Kendzior herself is whip smart, and her work is thoughtful, insightful, fascinating, meticulously researched, and downright frightening.

I also did a fair amount of research on the White House and the history of its construction and alterations over the years, including digging up all that I could about the Secret Service while safely quarantining myself away from the COVID-19 pandemic.

Obviously, a lot of information is classified and rightly so. One of the resources I found myself turning to most frequently in devel-

oping this story was the White House Museum website (http://www.
whitehousemuseum.org/), which I'm certain I visited almost daily
during the writing of this book.

Author and podcaster CE Albanese, a former US Secret Service
agent also proved to be an invaluable resource, thanks to his writ-
ings. His blog posts, "The Life of a Secret Service Agent" and "Secret
Service Agents Have Courage," helped develop the background of
Agent Mike Hutchinson and his fellow USSS officers. You can read
both of those posts on his website at http://www.cealbanese.com.
Another of Albanese's articles, "The Secret to Writing About the Secret Service," as published on CareerAuthors.com, yielded an abun-
dance of information on the lives and tools used by Secret Service
agents. You can read this piece online at http://careerauthors.com/
secret-writing-about-secret-service/.

In June, after news broke that President Trump had retreated
underground in the face of large protests outside the White House,
Caroline Delbert wrote "What We Know About the White House
Bunker" for *Popular Mechanics* (https://www.popularmechanics.
com/science/a32733175/white-house-bunker/). Delbert's article
provided me with a terrific starting point to learn more about the US
government's underground emergency shelters and the Deep Underground Command Center.

I was surprised by just how much information is readily acces-
sible to the public, but so much still remains hidden. Filling in the
blanks required a lot of imagination and guesswork, and I no doubt
made a number of mistakes. I certainly took plenty of liberties and a
healthy dose of artistic license for dramatic effect. Any errors in the
tactics and operations of the United States Secret Service and America's servicemen and servicewomen are entirely my own.

I've relied on the editorial team at Red Adept Editing for a num-

ber of my projects, and as usual, Stefanie Spangler Buswell did an incredible job helping me correct various issues with this manuscript. I'd like to thank her for her always-excellent editorial advice. Thanks, also, to Virge Buck, who proofread and added an extra level of polish to this project.

In addition to being an incredible author, Kealan Patrick Burke is also an extraordinary graphics designer. The cover gracing this book is all thanks to him. Kealan has done a number of excellent covers for me now, and somehow, he just keeps finding ways to top himself. I wish I could say the same about myself!

Thank you to you, too, for reading this book. I hope you enjoyed it, and your support means the world to me. I wouldn't be here without my loyal band of readers who help keep me going.

And, odd as it may sound, I have to offer ironic thanks to all those Trump voters out there, as well. If it weren't for them and Trump's constant assaults on our democracy these last four years, this book would not exist. As horror author Brian Keene said in a Facebook post (https://www.facebook.com/permalink.php?story_fb id=10154044086401398&id=189077221397) following the 2016 election, "Horror always does well in times of trouble," noting that Stephen King and *The Texas Chainsaw Massacre* "happened in the shadow of Watergate/Vietnam. Splatterpunk happened in the shadow of Reagan. Vertigo Comics happened in the shadow of Thatcher. My generation's success happened in the shadow of Bush Junior." Horror exists as a reaction to and against the authoritarian push of right-wing politics, and there's going to be a hell of a lot more horror to come in the shadow of Donald Trump and the Republican party's willing, loving embrace of fascism. Following Trump's victory, Keene told writers, "Go write about monsters and truth, because that's our job, and there's folks your age that are going to need it."

So, that's what I did here, and have been doing in other works, like *Revolver* and the Salem Hawley series, to some degree or another. I plan to keep on doing so.

Although I said it at the very front of this book, I think it bears acknowledgment once more here: thank you to everyone who voted against and helped to defeat Donald Trump in 2020. You saved this country and pulled us back from a real-life horror we might never have escaped. The fight, however, is far from over.

— November 12, 2020

A NOTE TO READERS

Thank you for choosing to read my work – it is greatly appreciated and I hope you enjoyed the journey.

If you would be willing to spare a minute or two, please leave a brief review of this work and let other readers know what you thought. Reviews are incredibly helpful, particularly for an independent author and publisher such as myself, and can help determine the success of a novel. Reviews do not need to be long – twenty words or so should suffice – but their impact can be enormous.

I look forward to your thoughts, and thank you, once again, for taking the time to read this story.

If you would like to know about upcoming releases, I encourage you to subscribe to my newsletter at http://michaelpatrickhicks.com.

ABOUT THE AUTHOR

Michael Patrick Hicks is the author of several horror books, including *The Resurrectionists*, *Broken Shells: A Subterranean Horror Novella*, and *Mass Hysteria*. He co-hosts Staring Into The Abyss, a podcast focused on all things horror. His debut novel, *Convergence*, was an Amazon Breakthrough Novel Award Finalist in science fiction. He is a member of the Horror Writers Association.

Michael lives in Michigan with his wife and two children. In between compulsively buying books and adding titles that he does not have time for to his Netflix queue, he is hard at work on his next story.

For more books and updates on Michael's work, visit his website: http://michaelpatrickhicks.com

CHECK OUT THESE
OTHER TITLES FROM

HIGH FEVER
BOOKS

THE SALEM HAWLEY SERIES: BOOK ONE

THE RESURRECTIONISTS

MICHAEL PATRICK HICKS

THE RESURRECTIONISTS

Having won his emancipation after fighting on the side of the colonies during the American Revolution, Salem Hawley is a free man. Only a handful of years after the end of British rule, Hawley finds himself drawn into a new war unlike anything he has ever seen.

New York City is on the cusp of a new revolution as the science of medicine advances, but procuring bodies for study is still illegal. Bands of resurrectionists are stealing corpses from New York cemeteries, and women of the night are disappearing from the streets, only to meet grisly ends elsewhere.

After a friend's family is robbed from their graves, Hawley is compelled to fight back against the wave of exhumations plaguing the Black cemetery. Little does he know, the theft of bodies is key to far darker arts being performed by the resurrectionists. If successful, the work of these occultists could spell the end of the fledgling American Experiment... and the world itself.

The Resurrectionists, the first book in the Salem Hawley series, is a novella of historical cosmic horror from the author of *Broken Shells* and *Mass Hysteria*.

THE SALEM HAWLEY SERIES: BOOK TWO

BORNE OF THE DEEP

MICHAEL PATRICK HICKS

BORNE OF THE DEEP

Emancipated during the American Revolution, Salem Hawley is a free man—until he finds himself indebted to a doctor for treatment for injuries incurred during the New York Doctors' Riot. Recruited to recover the stolen grimoire, *Al Azif*, Salem embarks on a journey north, to Arkham, Massachusetts.

Plagued by rain and the incursion of strange, otherworldly creatures, the seaside town of Arkham has become a dark and dangerous place. Unable to trust the locals, Hawley is forced to rely on only his wits to track down the thief. He must also contend with Louise LeMarché, an outcast and suspected witch who is searching for the missing tome, as well.

Time is against Hawley. Something ancient and evil is rising from the depths of the Atlantic, and if *Al Azif* is not recovered quickly, it could spell doom to Arkham... and all of humanity.

Borne of the Deep, the second book in the Salem Hawley series, is a novella of Lovecraftian cosmic horror and continues the story that began in *The Resurrectionists*.

AVAILABLE IN PRINT AND EBOOK

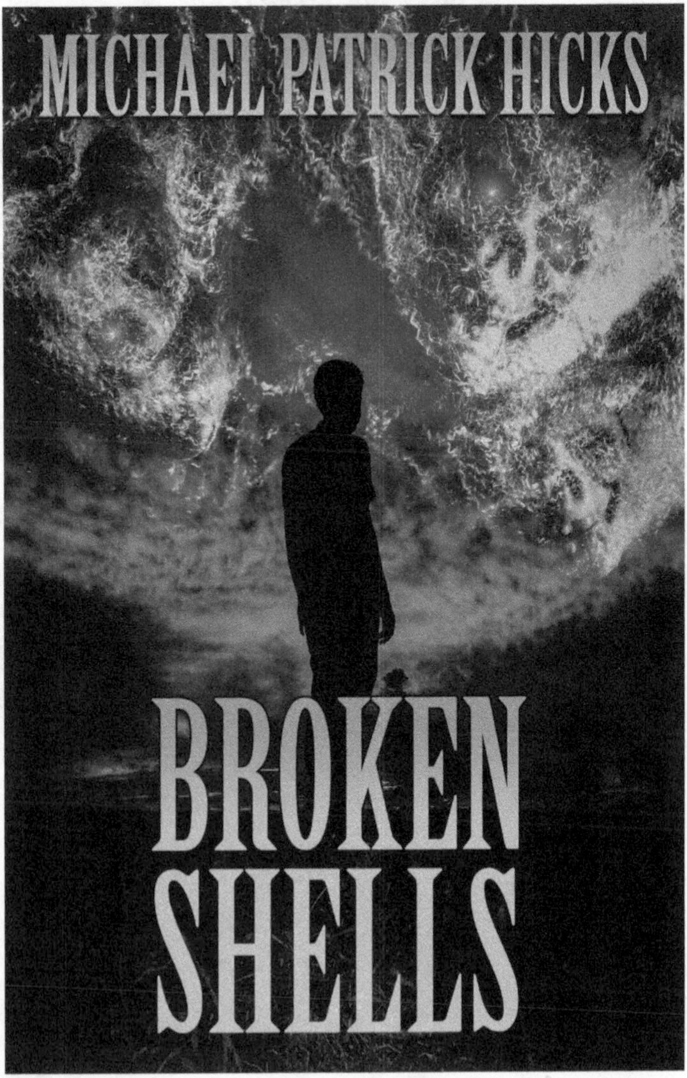

MICHAEL PATRICK HICKS
BROKEN
SHELLS

BROKEN SHELLS

Antoine DeWitt is a man down on his luck. Broke and recently fired, he knows the winning Money Carlo ticket that has landed in his mailbox from a car dealership is nothing more than a scam. The promise of five thousand dollars, though, is too tantalizing to ignore.

Jon Dangle is a keeper of secrets, many of which are buried deep beneath his dealership. He works hard to keep them hidden, but occasionally sacrifices are required, sacrifices who are penniless, desperate, and who will not be missed. Sacrifices exactly like DeWitt.

When Antoine steps foot on Dangle's car lot, it is with the hope of easy money. Instead, he finds himself trapped in a deep, dark hole, buried alive. If he is going to survive the nightmare ahead of him, if he has any chance of seeing his wife and child again, Antoine will have to do more than merely hope. He will have to fight his way back to the surface, and pray that Jon Dangle's secrets do not kill him first.

AVAILABLE IN PRINT, EBOOK, AND AUDIOBOOK

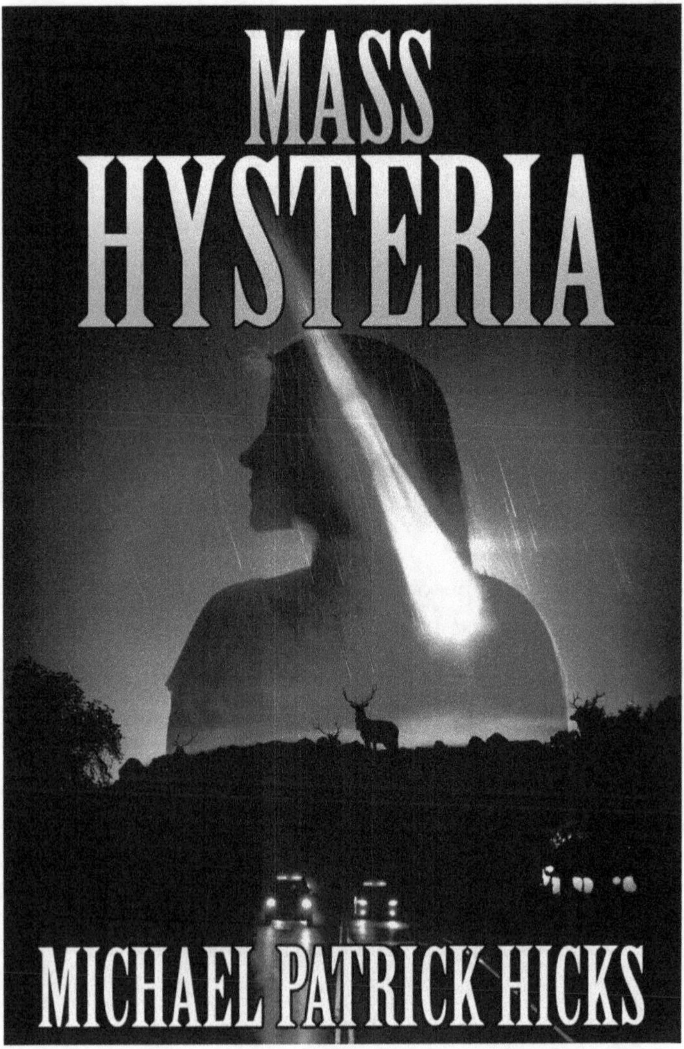
MASS
HYSTERIA
MICHAEL PATRICK HICKS

MASS HYSTERIA

It came from space...

Something virulent. Something evil. Something new. And it is infecting the town of Falls Breath.

Carried to Earth in a freak meteor shower, an alien virus has infected the animals. Pets and wildlife have turned rabid, attacking without warning. Dogs and cats terrorize their owners, while deer and wolves from the neighboring woods hunt in packs, stalking and killing their human prey without mercy.

As the town comes under siege, Lauren searches for her boyfriend, while her policeman father fights to restore some semblance of order against a threat unlike anything he has seen before. The Natural Order has been upended completely, and nowhere is safe.

...and it is spreading.

Soon, the city will find itself in the grips of mass hysteria.

To survive, humanity will have to fight tooth and nail.

AVAILABLE IN PRINT, EBOOK, AND AUDIOBOOK

REVOLVER

MICHAEL PATRICK HICKS

"A classic example of social science fiction"
David Wailing, Author of Auto

FOREWORD BY
LUCAS BALE

REVOLVER

The "stunning and harrowing" short story, originally published in the anthology No Way Home, is now available as a standalone release and features an all-new foreword written by award-winning science fiction author, Lucas Bale.

Cara Stone is a broken woman: penniless, homeless, and hopeless. When given the chance to appear on television, she jumps at the opportunity to win a minimum of $5,000 for her family.

The state-run, crowdfunded series, Revolver, has been established by the nation's moneyed elite to combat the increasing plight of class warfare.

There's never been a Revolver contestant quite like Cara before. The corporate states of America are hungry for blood, and she promises to deliver.

AVAILABLE NOW IN EBOOK AND AUDIOBOOK

"A sharp, crackling exploration of man's hubris and science gone wrong. This is Frankenstein for the new millennium."

HUNTER SHEA, author of We Are Always Watching and The Jersey Devil

MICHAEL PATRICK HICKS

BLACK SITE

BLACK SITE

FOR FANS OF H.P. LOVECRAFT AND ALIEN COMES A NEW WORK OF COSMIC TERROR!

Inside an abandoned mining station, in the depths of space, a team of scientists are seeking to unravel the secrets of humanity's origin. Using cutting-edge genetic cloning experiments, their discoveries take them down an unimaginable and frightening path as their latest creation proves to be far more than they had bargained for.

"A sharp, crackling exploration of man's hubris and science gone wrong. This is Frankenstein for the new millennium." — **Hunter Shea, author of We Are Always Watching and The Jersey Devil**

AVAILABLE NOW IN EBOOK AND AUDIOBOOK

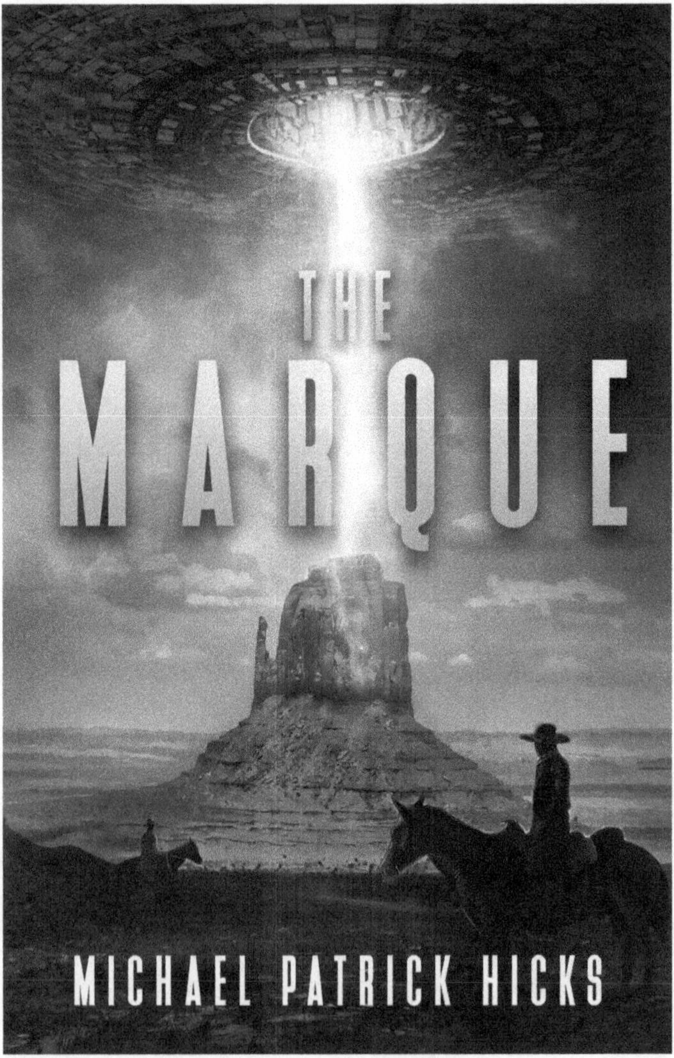
THE
MARQUE
MICHAEL PATRICK HICKS

THE MARQUE

The world has fallen beneath the rule of alien invaders. The remnants of humanity are divided into two camps: those who resist, and those serve.

Darrel Fines serves. He is a traitor, a turncoat who has betrayed his people, his wife, and most of all, himself. In this new world order, in which humanity is at the very bottom, Fines is a lawman for the violent and grotesque conquerors.

When the offspring of the Marque goes missing, Fines is charged with locating and recovering the alien. Caught in the crosshairs of a subdued worker's camp and the resistance cell that he was once allied with, Fines is forced to choose between a life of servility and a life of honor.

AVAILABLE NOW IN EBOOK

▬

For more titles and news about future releases, visit www.michaelpatrickhicks.com and subscribe to the mailing list.

<u>CONTENT WARNINGS</u>

Friday Night Massacre contains content that may be upsetting to some readers, including the following:

- Trumpism
- Racism
- Rape
- Sexual assault
- Incest
- Pedophilia
- Child abuse
- Child sexual abuse
- Infanticide
- Graphic violence

READER DISCRETION IS ADVISED

9 781947 570153